EAST OF THE
MISTY MOUNTAINS

AN OMF BOOK

© OVERSEAS MISSIONARY FELLOWSHIP
(formerly China Inland Mission)

Published by
Overseas Missionary Fellowship (IHQ) Ltd.,
2 Cluny Road, Singapore 1025, Republic of Singapore

First published 1991

OMF BOOKS are distributed by
OMF, 404 South Church Street, Robesonia, Pa 19551, USA
OMF, Belmont, The Vine, Sevenoaks, Kent, TN13, 3TZ, UK
OMF, PO Box 849, Epping, NSW 2121, Australia
OMF, 1058 Avenue Road, Toronto, Ontario M5N 2C6, Canada
OMF, PO Box 10159, Auckland, New Zealand
OMF, PO Box 41, Kenilworth 7745, South Africa
and other OMF offices.

ISBN 981-3009-12-8

Printed in Singapore
8K KHL 3/91

Contents

ONE
Lost

Fourteen-year-old Jeff Anderson inched cautiously towards the edge of the rocky ledge for a closer look. On all sides it was the same, fog-draped slopes, one silhouetted against another, fading into the white shroud below. Mountains appeared and vanished as the drifting mist swirled around them. Close at hand scrubby bushes and a wind-twisted pine tree scratched a living among clumps of rock.

Somewhere in the distance Jeff could hear a stream racing, and water was carving little tracks in the gravel around his sneakers. It must have rained here very recently.

But now only a drizzle misted the air, and fog enclosed him and the mountains in a water-logged sheet. Wind whipped around the peaks, adding biting chill to the dampness that was plastering Jeff's dark hair onto his forehead. He shivered. Must be wintertime. And here he was wearing only jeans and a light jacket, the neat white windbreaker that Aunt Nonie had given him for his birthday. Why did he ever let Uncle Zeke get him into these fixes?

Only a few minutes ago the lanky teenager had been in his Uncle Zeke's physics lab in Illinois. At the sprawling Fermi Lab, where Zeke worked, was a giant underground cyclotron. The mega-lab was used for many physics experiments. Researchers gravitated there from all over the world. Zeke himself was working on some kind of machine to spin protons around at speed high enough to fling them off into the distant reaches of space and time.

Jeff didn't understand the theory, really, but he'd heard his uncle talk about it often. In fact, the last time he visited Uncle Zeke and Aunt Nonie, he'd been caught in another of Zeke's experiments and ended up in Nineteenth-Century China. Of course, Zeke wouldn't believe that. Neither did Jeff's parents. The machine had misfired, they said — an experimental accident.

But this time, supposedly, the experiment was greatly improved. "We've really worked on this. Smoothed out the problems," Zeke had encouraged. "So you can choose your destination, both geographically and time-wise, much more accurately now. We've made a simplified formula for reversing the process too — bringing things back to the present again. So a particle being spun at high enough speeds could now, theoretically, be shot through space and time with accuracy to a chosen destination and retrieved at will."

Famous last words! Jeff should have known better than to let his uncle talk him into one more 'quick ride' in his experimental machine. *And now look where it got him!* he thought ruefully. *Here wherever this was!*

Jeff flattened his lean frame against the mountainside to protect himself from the wind and tried to figure out where he was. He was standing on a rocky ledge no more than three feet wide. A huge mountain loomed out of the thick mist in front of him. To his right a whole range of peaks marched on through the same mist to infinity. All Jeff could see on his left was the craggy profile of the mountain on which he stood. From the tips of his sneakers the terrain sloped sharply downwards and disappeared into the whiteness below. If a valley lay below him, his gray eyes couldn't see it. Fog swirled over the whole scene, clearing momentarily, moving one direction, then another, then advancing in greater density than ever before.

Where was he? With all these high, steep-sided mountain peaks everywhere, was he in the Alps maybe? How about the Rockies? No, the Rockies were West, and he had definitely chosen "East." He'd figure it out later. Meanwhile the cold was making his teeth chatter. He had to find someplace warm.

Where was the path? The ledge he was on was definitely no marked hiker's trail supervised by the Department of Parks and Recreation. In fact, it looked like people rarely came here. Maybe never. Maybe he was stranded on an inaccessible peak no one even knew about.

Jeff fought down a wave of panic. *Keep calm,* he told himself. *Think!* If there were any civilization, it was probably a long way below. He'd just have to head downwards. He was glad he'd chosen rappelling as an activity at camp one summer — though right now he could use a rope.

Here goes, Jeff thought and grabbed the rock jutting out from the cliff face to his left, turned to face the mountain, and lowered himself a few feet to a rock below.

Taking a deep breath, Jeff backed to the edge and felt cautiously with his toe for a stable spot below that would hold his weight. A few stones slithered away beneath his step. He shifted his foot a bit. There, that seemed to hold. Trembling, he shifted his weight slowly to that foot, then carefully tucked his other foot into the same toe-hold. Grabbing hold of a bush ahead of him, he reached his front leg down to seek footing for the next step.

This wasn't the same as at camp — the soil was looser, rockier, the mountainside scarier. Jeff could feel his heart pounding. Cold forced pain through his chest with every breath. The altitude, in fact, made him feel a bit light-headed.

Mustn't look down. One step, then another, Jeff encouraged himself. *Don't look, just move. Opps! Careful!* With the muscles already jumping in his legs, the stranded city kid swallowed the lump rising in his throat and tried to blot out everything but the next step.

But when he stopped for a breath, Jeff couldn't keep his mind from racing over and over the events of the last hour. The experimental thing had been fun at first. When his uncle had ushered his younger brother and him into the circular lab, the gravitational testing device looked exciting in its mustard-colored grandeur. A long, polished arm connected a truck-like cab to a heavy motor bolted to the floor. Inside, the cubicle reminded Jeff of a helicopter cockpit — dials, computer screens, joysticks, buttons, lights — a tiny cell with a padded seat and walls of hardware. He figured the experiment would involve some kind of super ride — like the "Whirling Whoopee" at the fair or something. Only very high-tech, of course.

With his brother watching, Jeff had climbed into the cockpit, and Zeke had explained some of the gadgets. Jeff knew he had been asked to choose "Forward" or "Back" for the time thrust, and he had chosen "Back." So this had to be somewhere in the past. And he had definitely turned the geographical selector dial "East," but after that it was all a blur.

Jeff closed his eyes and felt dizziness washing over him as he remembered. It was like being in the machine all over again. He felt the little cab rock back and forth and begin to spin rapidly. A hum filled his ears, and the atmosphere seemed to press against his face.

A few seconds later, Jeff remembered, he had suddenly felt his hand being thrown off the controls. Immediately he was flung back against the back of the seat with such force he could scarcely get his breath. He had yelled, grabbed frantically for a handhold, then had simply given way to the dizzying jumble of sensations cascading around him. Eventually the cubicle whirled so fast that it seemed to stand still. Jeff found himself shaking violently, his head feeling really weird. His whole body had a sensation of drifting apart. Spinning, spinning. And then nothing. The next thing he knew he had been dumped here on this mountainside.

Jeff had no idea how far back in time he'd gone, nor where in the world he'd landed — except that it had to be in the past and east of where he started.

Well, now Jeff had to concentrate on getting

down to a level where somebody lived. It was hard to judge how far he'd come. He couldn't turn his head back to see where he'd come from without losing his balance. Grabbing, clutching, feeling his way toehold by toehold, he lowered himself gradually down the steep side of the mountain.

His hands and feet were numb with cold now. The rain was penetrating his windbreaker, creeping into his sneakers, soaking his socks. He forced his toes to move even though he could hardly feel them.

Even if he did get safely down to more level ground, what then? Would anyone ever find him in this deserted spot? Just ahead he could see a huge rock the size of a table jutting out from the mountainside. Maybe from that point he could get a better view of things and decide what to do next.

More hopeful now, Jeff headed toward the rock. Cautiously he prodded the soggy ground with one foot, searching for a toehold. There — he'd gained a few feet. He reached out his right arm and grabbed at a tuft of coarse grass. It seemed solid. He pulled himself along. *Fingers frozen. Mustn't quit now. Mustn't stand still, press on, keep going. Inch by inch. Foot by foot.* His sneakers squished with water; every step took more will power to force movement from his icy toes. There, just ahead, was the big rock.

The rock top looked to be about five or six feet across, big enough to sit on, certainly. From its narrow base it reached out wedge-shaped over the chasm below. Underneath this roof-like over-hang, Jeff noticed a flat spot, wide enough for someone to sit, a spot that was almost dry and at least somewhat sheltered from the wind.

Maybe he wouldn't climb on top of the rock after all, Jeff rethought. He'd just pull himself over to it, then crawl underneath for a few minutes to get his bearings.

Wind whipped over the shivering hiker as he hesitated before moving crablike to the rock shelter. A stone slipped from under one foot. Another movement, and more stones scattered. A muddy ribbon of water rushed down the slope, getting stronger as it ran. The mist was becoming rain again now, and the wind seemed to increase.

Just then Jeff heard a muffled sound above him. High above the big rock, a boulder was break-ing away and beginning a destructive tumble down the mountainside. Suddenly what seemed like the whole mountaintop began to buckle and to slide, unchecked, down the slope.

More rocks joined in, and more, cutting a wider and wider path now as the avalanche gained momentum. Loose gravel flew, and the growing debris uprooted small bushes and swept them along.

Jeff froze for an instant. The mountain tumbled on, sweeping everything in its path. Suddenly he realized that the edge of the speeding rubble was coming straight towards him! His only hope was the protection offered by the rocky ledge. Desperately he made for the shelter, digging into the slope with his fingers and knees, clutching and clawing at anything that would hold his weight. Vaguely he was aware of a twig scratching his cheek as he pushed past it. The noise of the avalanche was like a cavalry approaching, marching right over his head.

Panting, he threw himself under the rocky overhang just as the first rocks crashed and tumbled around him. He scrambled into position, his back pressed firmly against the rock wall. With his hands he covered his face to protect it from flying dirt and stones.

Down the huge chunk of mountainside came, a stampede of earth, boulders, smaller rocks, bits of roots, bushes, loose gravel — debris of all sizes clattering onto the rocky roof overhead, crashing and scattering in a dozen different directions and racing down the slope to the bottom. Mud splashed in the slide's wake; gusts of wind turned the drizzle into momentary torrents of rain.

The avalanche lasted only a few minutes. The rocky hooves had galloped on by, and suddenly Jeff realized that it was quiet, that all he could hear above the wind and his pounding heart were a few loose stones tumbling into the chasm below.

Gradually the pounding in his chest died down,

and he caught his breath. His face stung, though.
A long scratch stretched from just below the bridge
of his nose to his earlobe.

Now Jeff realized again how cold he was, all
five-foot-seven of him shivering   uncontrollably.
He wasn't just cold, he was wet. Shoes, socks
and cuffs of his pants were soaked. His jacket
front was grubby and wet from pressing against
the mountainside.

As Jeff huddled under the rocky outcropping,
his scratched face stung with every jar of his
chattering teeth. He could feel only pain where
his fingers should be. He rubbed his hands together
briskly and put them in his pockets. No good.
He brought his hands to his mouth and puffed
several times. The warm breath condensed immediately on his cold skin, leaving them as icy as
ever.

Hypothermia! That's what was happening. He'd
read a story about hypothermia once in a scouting
magazine. The temperature wasn't so low, but
he was wet, and the wind was quickly evapo-
rating the dampness on his clothes and sucking
the heat from his body. People have been known
to freeze to death in conditions like this!

Well, that wasn't going to happen to him.
He'd never been a pessimist; this was no time
to start being one. No way he was going to die
on this stupid mountain! *You'll make it; keep
trying,* he told himself. *Just concentrate on*

getting out of here.

Taking a deep breath, Jeff sized up the situation. Under the huge rock he was completely closed in. Gravel lay in deep piles all around him. A boulder had jammed itself against the rocky over-hang, blocking the entrance way. Happily, since Jeff could see daylight around the jagged piece of granite, he knew at least he wouldn't suffocate while he worked on getting out.

The trapped boy tried shoving the wedged boulder with his shoulder. No use. He sat down facing the rock and pushed with both feet. It wouldn't budge. He kicked at the gravel on the left side. That rolled. He kept pushing, digging, kicking, every motion knocking away more loose stones. The activity helped to control his shivering.

There! — a hole opened with a small rush of air and a welcome burst of light. The fog seem-ed to be thinning. Jeff quickened his efforts to dig himself free, moving rocks with both hands now, jabbing with his feet when necessary. The opening got bigger. He managed to push one arm through it, dislodging one more rock and sending it down the precipice. Now a sizable pile of loose gravel fell away, leaving an opening Jeff judged big enough to crawl through. *Thank You, Lord,* he sighed gratefully, sticking his head out cautiously. If he could squeeze through and climb over the smaller rocks, he could get to the path.

Path? There hadn't been any path here when

he started out. But that certainly looked like one down on the rim below him. He'd been too busy picking his way along to look down before now, but now he saw it — a path, narrow perhaps, but a path. Good thing he was on the side of the slide where the path was headed downward.

Jeff felt more hopeful now. Somebody must come this way at least occasionally. If he could get to the trail, he could get help, surely. There had to be a police post or ranger station around — or something.

TWO

Written Nonsense

Jeff removed his wet shoes and socks, rubbed the circulation back into his toes and put his soggy footwear back on. Then he squeezed his body through the debris and crawled over the rocks to the trail below.

Walking was a little easier here. Still, the wind cut through Jeff's wet clothes like a blade of ice. He buried his fists in his jacket pockets. His fingers touched the hard, smooth plastic of his radio/cassette player.

A birthday gift from his parents, the radio/cassette player had all the things he'd wanted — a.m./f.m. radio, three-band equalizer, auto-reverse, headphones plus speaker at the back if desired, and it could record as well as play. Besides all that, sunlight would recharge its batteries. He knew his folks had paid plenty for the compact instrument.

Jeff had stuffed the radio/cassette player into his pocket after showing it to Zeke and Nonie that morning. He was mad at himself for bringing it along. Wouldn't do him any good here; there was probably no such thing as a radio station for miles. Of course, he could always play the one cassette he had in it — Cray Temple's new album, "River."

But how would he explain the radio/cassette player to anyone in this forsaken place, especially if he was far back in history? No, it was better to keep it hidden, at least for the time being.

Jeff trudged on. Suddenly he stubbed his toe on a hidden chunk of granite in the path. His half-frozen big toe screamed with pain, and Jeff hobbled a few feet on one squishy foot, his face twisting in sympathy. Ow! This was hardly the kind of adventure he was looking for. Miserable, that's what it was, miserable! He was used to city life in Minnesota, where his dad was a surgeon, his mom a newspaper writer — normal American life. This was too much! Good thing he wouldn't have to stay here long, wherever it was. Zeke would probably be working on his re-entry right now.

As he rounded a bend, Jeff was suddenly alert as his eyes followed the path to a collection of tiny huts in the distance. Too far away to be

clear in detail, the huts were at least a sign of
life. Jeff tried to hurry, but he was too stiff with
cold.

As the cluster of shacks came into better view,
Jeff saw that they were unevenly scattered up
and down the hillside, maybe fifty or sixty of them.
That's all you could call them — a cluster of
shacks. Not a town, that's for sure. Hardly even
a village. There wasn't a decent building in the
bunch — but low, gray structures hugging the
mountainside. One of them, at least, was propped
up on one side by doubtful-looking poles. Most
looked to Jeff as if a puff of wind might send
them toppling into the valley below.

This didn't exactly seem like China. Didn't look
like anywhere he'd ever seen, in fact. Tibet maybe.
Pictures of Tibet always looked like this. Maybe
he was in the Himalayas.

The chickens, who had been scratching hopefully along the mud path, scattered as Jeff approached. At the last moment a skinny dog, who
had been sleeping under one of the nearer houses,
lifted his head from a muddy foreleg to let out
a bark, high-pitched and nervous.

At first Jeff saw no human inhabitants. The
houses were basically alike, their walls made of
woven split bamboo, their sloping roofs made of
dried thatch tied in place with thongs of bamboo.
Each structure was sitting on just enough flattened
ground to allow a tiny yard. Inside a pen beside

the porch of the closest house, a large black pig grunted and nosed about. A garden plot no bigger than his bedroom produced some kind of greens.

Jeff hesitated. What should he do now? Just then a girl he judged to be about eleven or twelve came to the door, baby jostling on one hip. Behind her was a younger child, probably also a girl, Jeff guessed. Both girls were dressed in dark blue with colored stripes around their skirts. Wide turbans formed a brim around their heads, hiding most of their uncombed charcoal-black hair.

The older girl also wore an apron over her skirt, decorated with beads or shells of some kind. She had the same sort of beads dangling down each side of her face. They didn't seem to be earrings, exactly. They seemed rather to be attached to the turban on her head. The decorations clacked and jingled with every motion of the girl's body. The name, Jingles, popped immediately into Jeff's mind. Both Jingles and the little sister she cared for were filthy — hands, hair, faces, bare feet all unwashed. And the baby, besides being dirty, had a runny nose. *Yuck!* thought Jeff.

The children stared at Jeff openly. The older girl fastened her gaze on Jeff's eyes, her own widening in a confused fear. *Probably thinks I'm a ghost,* thought Jeff. He smiled.

After a moment a shy smile lit up the older girl's face, and the younger girl immediately copied her. The little one ducked behind her sister shyly.

No one said a word, just looked.

Suddenly, without taking their eyes off Jeff, the girls began to jabber loudly, alerting the woman Jeff presumed to be their mother, who came to the doorway and stared too. She was dressed just like "Jingles" and wasn't much cleaner.

By this time heads popped out from houses around. Children poured out of doorways and stood staring — some wide-eyed and uncertain, some giggling behind grubby hands, some venturing remarks. Jeff felt like a monkey in a zoo.

Well, now that the village people had seen him, Jeff couldn't just walk away. Besides, he needed to get warm, and even a bamboo house might be better than nothing. He walked closer to the flimsy woven wall, not knowing what to expect, and spoke to the woman standing at the doorway: "Hello. I'm Jeff Anderson." It sounded too formal, sort of dumb, but Jeff plowed on desperately, "Could you help me? I'd like to come in and get warm."

No response. The woman looked blank. Jeff felt more and more awkward as the villagers stared, chattered, laughed, and pointed. Obviously they didn't understand what he said. Of course not. But he would have to make them understand some way before he froze to death or died of hunger.

Jeff, feeling very white despite his own grubbiness, shivered exaggeratedly and hugged himself tightly, rubbing his arms vigorously with his hands. He rubbed his stomach and moved his hand up and down to his mouth as if eating. Universal sign for food, he hoped. Anyway, he had to try something.

The mother turned and went inside. *Oh no! Couldn't she see he needed help? What more —?* Oh, the girl with the baby was looking at him, turning to the door like she expected him to follow. She motioned him closer with her arm and repeated whatever it was she had just said. Maybe she meant "Come in." Jeff watched a moment longer, then decided that she expected him to enter. Good, they got his message.

Here goes! Jeff thought and ducked through the doorway. Immediately he was plunged into near blackness. The only distinguishable sensation at first was the sharp, acid smell of smoke burning his nose and eyes. A small open fire glowed from the earthen floor. There were no windows, light from outside managing to squeeze in only through the door and pinpoint holes in the bamboo wall. Looked like one room, with maybe another one off behind — he couldn't tell for sure. The whole house wasn't as big as their living room at home.

The smoke twining up from the fire made Jeff's eyes water. *How can they breathe in here?* Jeff wondered. Walls, floor, clothes, all seemed covered with soot and grime. No wonder Jingles and her family were dirty!

Jeff stepped in further as his eyes adapted to the darkness. The only pieces of furniture were three low crudely made stools and a log placed near the fire. Otherwise, except for a couple of black pots, one on a metal tripod over the fire, some wooden cooking utensils, and an assortment of bins and baskets in one corner, the room was bare. Stiffly Jeff lowered himself onto the log.

Immediately the children squatted down beside him, not on the log, but on their heels, their feet flat on the dirt floor. They looked as comfortable as he would be if he were sprawled on the rug at home. He could use a little of that comfort right now!

The heat from the open fire quickly began to penetrate Jeff's body, however, and eventually even his fingers and toes reluctantly responded. Trouble was his feet ached as the circulation came back into them. He wiggled his toes inside his steaming shoes to try to take away the hurt. His clothes and hair steamed too. A bit more of this and he'd be well-done and ready for eating, at least on one side.

Eating! The idea came to him with new force. Now that he was not as concerned with preventing hypothermia, he realized how hungry he was.

But eat here? Not likely. For one thing, it didn't look like there was anything much to eat. And for another, he didn't relish putting anything in his mouth that came from a place as dirty as this. It would be crawling with germs. Even worms, maybe. Who knows what? No, he couldn't eat here.

But where on earth else was he going to find *anything* to eat? He realized now that, beautiful as this area was, this was no tourist resort. No pizza place or a hamburger joint around the next curve here! No way to phone out for anything either. He'd better take what he could get.

Encouragingly the lady was stirring something in the pot on the fire. When it seemed to be done to her satisfaction, she lifted the kettle of food to the side of the fire area, presumably to sit and steam while a second black pot was settled on the fire. Jeff closed his eyes; the smell that wafted toward him as the second kettle began to puff steam was not bad, not bad at all. Oh, was he hungry!

The chattering of the children around him made him open his eyes. With a dipper created from a gourd, the woman was ladling something into a bowl. She picked up two chopsticks from the palm leaf they were lying on, and handed the whole place setting to Jeff. The bowl was filled with steaming rice, a hard boiled egg and something that looked like cabbage, not normally his favorite food. He took the food, and said thank you.

Maybe his hostess could tell by his smile and nod that he appreciated the meal. Anyway he would have to try it. Couldn't hurt her feelings.

And he was hungry.

Cautiously he lifted a bite to his mouth, glad he'd learned to manage chopsticks. The food had a smoked flavor, but besides that it tasted like rice and cabbage and an egg. Not bad. *Just don't think about what else may be crawling in it,* he told himself. *Just eat! Tastes okay,* he decided and put another bite into his mouth. And another. The children watched him, smiling, pointing and chattering as he ate. Before he knew it the bowl was empty.

While Jeff ate, Jingles sat watching him curiously. Besides examining the seams down the sides of his jeans, she seemed to be sizing him up, wondering if he could be trusted. *No wonder,* he thought, scratched and wet as he was, he probably looked pretty grim. Somehow his now-scuffed Reeboks looked out of place.

As the bedraggled Jeff finished his meal, "Jingles" seemed to have made a decision. She said something to her mother and slipped over to one of the baskets in the corner and returned with a piece of paper. She handed it to Jeff. All the family stood quietly waiting while Jeff looked at it. They seemed to be expecting something.

Jeff looked at the paper in front of him. It was written in English letters all right, but some of them were upside down or backwards. He couldn't read it. It made no sense at all. He smiled faintly, nodded, and looked at the girl.

"This doesn't say anything. I don't know where on earth you got it, but it doesn't mean anything to me." Immediately the family began chattering again. Though they obviously wanted some information, he didn't know what to say.

He shrugged his shoulders and set the paper down on the log beside him.

Just then, from the house next door came the sound of shouting. Other voices joined in, all seemingly in a rage, as if a fight was in progress. Jeff glanced up at the lady as she grabbed the baby and clutched him tightly in her arms. She was looking at the doorway, and her face was marked with terror.

Suddenly a man burst through the doorway and stomped over to where Jeff was standing. He was heavy for his height, almost square with his loose blue quilted jacket and baggy pants. His fat feet bulged over black satin shoes.

But what captured Jeff's attention was the anger that hardened every feature of the wide, lobster-colored face. He shouted at the family, waving his long stick around as he spoke. Jeff didn't need to understand the words to tell he was angry. He ducked as the speaker's stick knocked over a pot and came swooping toward him. All of a sudden the man's black, glinting eyes spotted the piece of paper lying on the log.

The hulking visitor picked up the paper with obvious interest. For a moment all was quiet as he turned it over and over, trying to make sense of the words written on it. Jeff held his breath. In a moment the man shouted again, this time directing his anger to Jeff. His face flashed rage; he jabbed a brown finger at the paper, then at Jeff, yelled again at the whole household and marched out the door. The paper was still crumpled in the palm of his hand.

Jeff let out his breath cautiously. The girl and her mother whispered in a burst of tense, frightened tones. The baby wailed, and the mother joggled it absent-mindedly. Through the doorway Jeff could see the intruder mount a skinny horse, crack a whip and ride off. A toothpick of a man, as thin as the horse, shuffled anxiously alongside.

"Whew!" Jeff said, "what was that all about?" Whatever it was, the fat man seemed to think Jeff was part of it, though he hadn't even done anything! Jeff realized he was shaking from head to toe, not from the cold this time. To get himself together, he sat down again on the log beside the fire.

Don't worry about that guy, he told himself. *I'll never see him again. He doesn't know me. He has no way of finding me. Besides, I won't be here long enough to be in any danger. Zeke'll buzz me home in a few minutes. He's got the experiment a lot better controlled this time.*

Gradually Jeff stopped shivering. Now what? He was warmer, certainly, and getting dry. And he'd had a pretty good meal, for now anyway. He couldn't stay here forever. All those pairs of dark eyes looking at him made him uneasy. Only sensible thing to do was to get up and get walking.

The family seemed anxious about his going. They smiled, but there was fear in their eyes as they stood at the doorway watching him leave. He headed on down the narrow trail.

On the side of the path, lodged against a rock, Jeff spotted a crumpled piece of paper. It was the page of odd writing Jingles had shown him. He studied it again. Uh-uh. No sense. He folded it carelessly and stuck it in his pocket.

There seemed to be no sign of the intruder and his servant. Jeff hoped they were far ahead of him and would turn off somewhere.

THREE

Answers and Accusations

Sunshine was poking its fingers through the fog that hovered just above Jeff's head. At its warm touch, the haze retreated and the white billows that shrouded the valley below parted to give Jeff a view. Colored by shadow as well as sunshine, mountain peaks loomed gray, then lavender, then green or many shades of blue.

Jeff enjoyed the walk now that he'd had something to eat and his clothes were almost dry. But it was still not warm. Wind whistled then vanished, to appear again a minute later, in a howling game of tag. Every gust of wind raised goosebumps; each warm patch of sunshine smoothed them out.

Jeff pushed aside a pine branch that nearly blocked his path as he picked his way among exposed tree roots. Trees were taller and thicker here. No telling where he was going. Eventually, surely, he'd come to a bigger place, a city maybe, and someone who spoke English.

Where in the world was he? It was crazy not knowing where he was or when it was. Who were those people back there in the village notched into the mountainside? Black-eyed and black-haired, with their light brown skin and round, flat faces, they looked Asian. Not exactly like Chinese, at least not like the Chinese he'd known. Eskimos probably looked like that, but neither the costumes nor the mountains seemed just right. Anyway, he had definitely selected East when he chose location in that flight simulator gismo. This had to be Asia.

There was no way of telling from the surroundings what year it was. Last month or a century ago. From the looks of that village, it could be a thousand years ago. Oh, brother! If it were too long ago, it would be hard to explain how he got here. Even an English speaker, if he found one, wouldn't have any idea what he was talking about if he told about Uncle Zeke's experiment.

Suddenly Jeff stopped. A blue speck bobbed and jolted on the hillside ahead and to his left. Jeff blinked and shielded his eyes from the sun. It appeared again. It was, he could see now, a rider on horseback. A second rider followed a short distance behind.

The way the two men were coming, it seemed likely that Jeff and the riders would soon cross paths. Maybe these two could help him. On second thought, if they weren't any friendlier than the last stranger he'd met, he'd better hide and hope they didn't see him. As they were coming around a bend and were still some distance away, Jeff had time to get a good view of the riders before being seen himself.

The first man, carrying only a small saddlebag and a blanket roll, rode easily in the saddle, his whole body moving in fluid rhythm with the animal under him. He was dressed like a Chinese, but looked more like a peasant than a wealthy man. He must be tall, however, for his feet hung far below the horse's belly; his thin frame looked as if it would unfold to at least six feet.

When the two riders were close enough, Jeff got a good look at the second rider. Shorter, he was dressed in dark blue jacket and oversized turban, not unlike those worn in the villages Jeff had just seen.

Now and then the wind seemed to carry the sound of music Jeff's way. Just a few notes. Then it disappeared again in the wind. Closer now, Jeff heard it again, distinctly this time. Yes, it was music, the sound of a man's voice, no doubt about it. Where was it coming from?

Jeff's curiosity increased as the odd-looking couple approached. The first man appeared to have something propped up in front of him, sort of attached to the saddle horn — a paper or book of some kind. Was he reading as he rode?

As Jeff watched, the man took one hand off the rein to wave it up and down in the air, finger pointing as he did so, like a music director. The humming had risen to a full-throated song now with a deliberate flourish at the end to match the arm motions. Suddenly Jeff realized what was going on. The man had music in front of him and was humming and beating it out as he went along. The absent-minded conductor didn't seem concerned that his horse could easily jostle him off as it picked its way over the mossy rocks, or that the beast could slip suddenly off the path, throwing his human cargo into the canyon below.

Jeff could hear what the man was humming. It was a piece Jeff had had in one of his piano books — one he'd practiced long and hard for several weeks, as a matter of fact. What was that tune? Yeah, the Russian Dance from the Nutcracker Suite by Tchaikovsky — that's what it was!

There was an unreal quality about the whole scene — a Chinese peasant riding a horse, playing classical music to himself! Jeff shook his head and ran his fingers through his hair vigorously as if to clear his thinking.

The men were so close that Jeff knew he was not going to be able to stay out of sight. He'd have to meet these two, act friendly and try to make them understand that he needed help.

Jeff came to the junction just as the other two rode up. The first rider pulled his horse to a halt. Jeff saw immediately that this 'Chinese peasant' was actually a Westerner, not only tall but blond. In front of him, propped up against the horse's neck, was some sheet music.

The white man was not smiling, and his long, deeply creased face seemed to reflect a no-nonsense spirit. The tall stranger seemed unaware of his disheveled appearance, his Chinese jacket wrinkled and baggy and his loose-fitting pants hardly reaching his ankles. *Awesome!* was the first word that came to Jeff's mind.

Yet when the blue-eyed horseman dismounted and extended his hand, Jeff detected such a warmth about him and such a sparkle in his eyes that the fourteen-year-old immediately felt at ease.

"Hello, there. What are you doing here? May I help you?"

Jeff gulped. The man spoke English. Relief suddenly washed over him, and words tumbled out: "Yes, you can. Well, I mean, I'm Jeff, Jeffrey Anderson. I got here by mistake, and I'd like to know where I am and how to get to a city or somewhere so I can get home."

"Pleased to meet you, Jeffrey. I'm J. O. Fraser, James Fraser. I'm from England myself, but I live here," he threw a nod toward the east, "that is, a few days from here. I'll be glad to do what

I can for you. And this is my friend, Ba Thaw."

The second rider, not a Westerner, flashed a warm smile, reached out and grabbed Jeff's hand in a firm grasp. "How do you do, Jeffrey?"

"You — you speak English too?" Jeff asked stunned. *Stupid,* he told himself. *You know he does; you just heard him.*

"Yes." The man laughed gently. "Surprised? I am of the Karen tribe, but I've been working for the British government in Burma. My English is enough to get along." An understatement, Jeff thought as he returned his handshake. This man's smile was big enough to make up for the sober expression of his companion. Another gust of wind made Jeff's teeth chatter.

"You're cold. Here — I've got an extra coat here somewhere." The lanky Westerner dismounted and opened the saddle bag, taking out a handful of papers and a small jar and finally pulling out a blue jacket. It was like the one the tribesman was wearing, rough and certainly too big for Jeff, but it would work well over his own white jacket.

Jeff slipped his arms into the homespun coat gladly. "Thanks. Thanks very much. It's freezing up here. Where are we, anyway?"

"About 5000 feet above sea level up near the Burma border."

"Burma?"

"Well, we're actually in China right here, in Yunnan Province. West China. But these mountains form the border. Burma's over that way. I've just come from there." J.O.Fraser pointed off to the endless peaks to the right. "And further over there to the west are the Himalayas."

"Wow. So that's where we are! I stopped in that village back there and got warmed up. They gave me something to eat too. But I didn't have any idea where I was."

"This village you stopped in — tell me about it." Fraser's face suddenly came to life.

Jeff described the place and location. Fraser and Ba Thaw looked at each other and nodded. "You must have stopped at Mottled Hill. I've visited there."

Jeff hesitated before asking his next question, "Ah, one more thing ... what's the date?"

Mr. Fraser looked at Jeff with an odd smile. "Date? I'm not sure. Let's see, we left Burma on the twelfth. This must be the fifteenth or sixteenth — January sixteenth." Jeff waited breathlessly. *What year? Add the year!* he pleaded silently. *Please don't make me ask what year it is!*

Mr. Fraser looked at him oddly. Then as if he sensed the boy's confusion, he added, "1915, of course. What's the matter? Lose a few days somewhere?" Obviously the accent was some sort of British.

Okay, that's better, Jeff thought. *So I've landed in China about 75 or 80 years ago.* What did that mean? No time-travel back then, that's for sure. No jets. Not even trains, maybe, away back here. Telephones? What about cars?

"Uh, yeah, I guess so. Yeah, just lost track of the date, you know how it is." He tried to smile casually. No sense telling him he'd lost track of the year, the century, the continent, the whole bit! He'd never be able to explain!

"Where're you from?" asked J. O., obviously puzzled at the jeans Jeff was wearing, faded, yet looking almost new. And those patched and padded shoes . . . .

"Minnesota. Uh ... that's in the United States. About a day's drive from Chicago, where I was born. Ever heard of it?"

"Chicago, sure. I had a coworker here a few months ago who trained in Moody Bible Institute in Chicago. Carl Gowman, his name was. But, let me see, I can't think of anyone I know who's from Minnesota, just off hand. What does your father do there?"

"My father's a surgeon, heart surgeon," answered Jeff, wishing that his father could meet this eccentric, but neat guy. "My mother works too — she's a writer for the Minneapolis *Star and Tribune.*"

"I see," responded the man, his face frowning as questions outstripped answers. "Are they in China with you?"

Jeff found his fingers naturally burrowing their way into his hair the way they always did when he got nervous. He swallowed before he answered,

as easily as he could, "Uh, no. No, they're not."
He pursed his lips together and shrugged one
shoulder. "I'll be seeing them pretty soon."

Fraser's intense eyes peered into him, but he
dropped the subject for now. "United States. Hmm.
That's one place I'd like to visit. My grandfather
lived in Canada for a time. I hope to go back
some day. Have you seen the new — what would
you call it, building, statue, structure — the memorial
to Lincoln that Henry Bacon designed last year?
I hear it's a beautiful piece of architecture. In
Washington, D.C., isn't it?"

Jeff tried to squelch the surprise in his voice.
"Oh, the Lincoln Memorial. Yeah, yeah I've seen
it. Yes, it's very nice. How did you hear about
it?" This guy was amazing.

"Oh, I keep up with things. I may live like
a Chinese peasant, but I'm not totally out of touch."
Fraser hoisted his long-legged frame back on to
his horse, giving the animal an encouraging pat,
and they moved on slowly down the path. "My
mother sends me newspapers from time to time.
I read every sentence I can get my hands on."
Fraser laughed as he added, "In fact, I even follow
the American baseball scores! What d'you think
about Boston's winning the World Series last
summer? Were you cheering for Boston?"

Jeff wanted to ask who else was playing, but
he didn't dare display his ignorance. He smiled
and shrugged, "I guess so."

"From the stories about it, it must have been a good series. My brother told me all the details. Boston all the way. Four to zero. I really hoped Philadelphia would have won at least one game. I'm kind of partial to the American League, myself."

Jeff smiled and answered quickly, "Oh, yeah, me too." This man keeps up with what's happening in America? Out here? That would be the World Series of 1914.

He looked down at his now-scuffed sneakers. *Don't suppose they had Reeboks back then,* he mused. Wet and bedraggled with his face scratched like it was, he was suddenly aware of his suspicious appearance. He felt uneasy about Mr. Fraser's eyes on him — Fraser wasn't easily fooled. But whatever he might have thought, at least he wasn't asking too many questions. Jeff hurried to change the subject.

The rain had made the rocks slippery, and the rushing streams darting here and there constantly dislodged small areas of rock and soil. As the trio moved down the trail, Jeff had to grab at the clumps of bushes to keep his balance, and several times he stumbled. Ba Thaw seemed not to notice. Jeff marveled at the way the Karen man in his neat tribal clothes and broad smile treated each obstacle as a mere minor inconvenience.

And James Fraser was just like him. He pushed onward, dismounting when the path was too treacherous, clambering over rocks, picking himself up when he fell down, pulling his feet out of ankle-deep mud in another place. He seemed to take it for granted that traveling was always like this.

"Some trails!" Jeff mumbled. "Does it ever get better?"

"Oh, yes, when we get closer to town. Once we get down on the plain it'll even out, and walking will be easier."

Town —that sounded good. So there was civilization around here some place.

"So, where're you going?" He directed the question at the tall, thin man strolling along beside him, loosely holding his horse by the reins.

"I'm headed for Tantsah. I've been in Burma for a few weeks working with Ba Thaw, and he's been good enough to accompany me this far. He'll head back soon, but I'm going on to settle at Tantsah." He beat out the final few bars of his music with one finger, humming as he did so. Then as if again remembering Jeff was there, he asked, "Where are you headed? You can't just wander around here all by yourself. Why don't you come with me? There's always room for one more."

"Thank you." Jeff nodded. He didn't know this man at all, but it was the best offer he'd had since arriving at the end of the world. And when you're desperate enough — "Okay, I'll do that.

I won't be here long, but thanks."

Suddenly the desire to go back home seemed overwhelming. He'd find a way to get back, of course. Maybe Fraser could help.

Jeff cleared his throat and wondered how to approach the subject. What could he expect in 1915? His new companions probably wouldn't be able to help him. They wouldn't know anything about computer-generated simulation. Maybe there weren't even planes flying to America. Oh, what a mess he'd gotten himself into!

"Here, get on my horse for a while. You look beat. I'll walk." Fraser folded up the music and replaced it in his saddlebag, gave Jeff a boost, and then gently led the horse down the twisted, narrow trail.

Jeff was glad for the ride. It was all he could do to walk without slipping. He wondered how the animal could carry a passenger on his back on a track like this.

As they wound their way down the steep slope, Jeff asked some of the questions lurking in his mind. "So what are you here for?" Jeff addressed James Fraser. "I mean, a job, sightseeing, what?"

"I'm a missionary. I've been here about four years. Came from England. I'm with an organization called the China Inland Mission."

Jeff gulped. China Inland Mission! That was the group Hudson Taylor had started, the group he'd met last time he'd traveled in Zeke's time machine and landed in China. He never expected to run into them again. He almost asked how Hudson Taylor was, and Maria and the children and his friend Duncan, but he stopped himself. Besides that was too long ago — 1867. Taylor and Maria and the others might be dead by now.

Fraser's voice brought him back to the moment. "There's a group of us working in China, not all in this rugged area, mind you. Some of the rest have more sense! They stay down at a human altitude instead of trying to compete with the mountain goats."

Ba Thaw laughed heartily. "But the mountain goats get to enjoy the view!"

"D'you like it up here?" he asked, wondering what his parents would think if they could see the characters he was traveling with.

"Like it? I love it!" Fraser answered, pointing a long finger across the canyon. "Just look at that view. Gorgeous! Nothing else like it on earth. I love mountains. And I love exploring, roughing it a bit, that sort of thing. You know, in the summers my cousin Aleck and I used to go to Switzerland and climb together. We loved it. But it was nothing compared to this. This is the life for me."

Fraser broke into a hum again, and Jeff said nothing.

"Ba Thaw and I have had quite a trip." Fraser shifted his bag slightly. "Burma's beautiful. We spent one night on top of the range, about 10,000 feet up! Talk about a view! Snowed a good three inches that night." He pulled a packet of some kind of plain cookies from his saddlebags and handed them around, helping himself to three before he continued.

"Ba Thaw had never seen snow before. We had to cross the pass in it, and almost got lost."

"We also met some robbers," Ba Thaw continued. "Armed too. But they didn't attack us. I guess they were waiting for wealthier prey. Wise!" He chuckled.

Jeff shuddered. He made robbers sound like a common inconvenience along the road, sort of like a stone in your shoe. "Robbers? Is robbery common?"

"It's not the first time that it happened to us."

"Did you walk? All the way to Burma?" Jeff couldn't believe these two.

Mr. Fraser just laughed. "All the way. And back. Until we picked up these two tired old nags at a village two days ago. Even so we have to walk a good deal of the time. Besides, I like walking."

Jeff looked at Fraser's long legs striding easily alongside, even though he must have been walking for hours already. *He must have developed some fantastic leg muscles,* Jeff thought.

Fraser continued, "Mr. Tsai, a Christian from Tantsah area came with me part of the way. He stopped at Three Rivers to buy salt."

Ba Thaw spoke up, grinning, "Mr. Fraser says he came to Burma to work with me on a project." The Karen man paused to chuckle, "— actually he came because he wanted English cooking and a hot bath."

Fraser agreed, laughing. "I won't deny it. Burma seems sophisticated after tramping around up here for months. I love it here. I even love rough, outdoor living when I have to, but I haven't forgotten how to enjoy luxury when I get a chance."

"You must be a good pianist. I mean ... playing music as you ride along."

Fraser smiled. "Oh you noticed that, did you? Well, I like to have music in front of me to 'listen to,' so to speak. My sister and I used to ride our bicycles up to London just to hear a symphony. Still enjoy a good concert when I have a chance."

Ba Thaw laughed and winked at Jeff. "J. O.'s too modest. He's actually a very accomplished concert pianist. He 'hears' music even on paper!"

A concert pianist — dressed like that and living out here in the middle of nowhere? It blew his mind. "I play the piano a little bit," Jeff said for want of anything better to say. Suddenly he grabbed the horse's mane as the animal lurched a bit in picking its way over the rocks, almost bouncing his rider off.

After a few minutes Jeff asked, "Does anybody live this far up? I mean more than just the village I saw when I first lan—when I first arrived. Are there any real towns or anything?"

"No, but thousands of Lisu."

"What?"

"Lisu people. See, although the bigger towns on the flat plains are thoroughly Chinese, most of the people here on these mountains are not Chinese, but Lisu. A tribe. They speak Lisu. They dress differently, live differently. Lisu villages are scattered all over these mountains. Like that one you saw, for instance — Mottled Hill Village."

"So this place you're going — is it a Lisu village?"

"Tantsah? No, not exactly but there are a lot of Lisu living there and in the surrounding area. Like Mr. Tsai, for instance. He's from Six Family Hollow, and he's one of the first Lisu — in spite of his Chinese name — to become a Christian. His whole family believed in Christ when I visited them a few years ago." Fraser stepped over a fallen tree and held it down for Jeff to follow. "Tantsah is a significant center to the Lisu. That's why it's important to get a group of Christians established there as examples, leaders, so other Lisu will follow."

"Is it a big place?"

"About a hundred families."

Jeff's heart sank. Only a hundred families! Maybe, what, five hundred people? There were three times as many as that in his high school back home in Rochester. He'd hoped this man would lead him to a city where he could find a way home. And here he was going to settle in a village of 500 people!

"Do Mr. Tsai and the Christians in Tantsah know you're coming? Have they got a house for you to live in?" Jeff thought of the hut he had just been in. If that was any example of what Mr. Fraser was getting into —

"Yes. I've got a great little place there. I was living there for a few weeks before I left for Burma, and they all asked me to come back and live there again."

Well, that sounded encouraging at least. "A great little place," he said. Of course, it seemed this man's idea of "great" wasn't quite the same as most people's, judging from what Jeff had seen so far. Even so, he must have a regular house, anyhow — with a bathroom, running water, beds, kitchen — the usual things a person needs. Jeff felt more comfortable already. The sooner they got there, the better.

As the path was slippery here, Jeff got off the horse to let the beast pick his way over rocks that had fallen across the path. Mud squeezed out from under each hoofprint. Though the mist had fallen and covered the path again, the trail was wider and smoother now as they descended quickly to the valley floor. Jeff mounted again and found himself nodding off to sleep as the horse's gait took on an even rhythm.

The sun was sinking over the other side of

the sky when Jeff saw what Mr. Fraser pointed out — two men on the path ahead. They had no baggage and no horses, and they seemed to be in a hurry. They came directly to Mr. Fraser, almost running, greeted him briefly and then began to talk excitedly, in tense tones. Only a slight tension to Fraser's mouth gave any sign of his reaction.

"Oh-oh," Ba Thaw said, overhearing the conversation. "Doesn't sound good." When the Karen tribesman went over to join the new-comers, Jeff sat on a roadside rock watching the interchange.

After half an hour or so the messengers turned and went back the way they had come. Mr. Fraser sat down beside Jeff, his long legs stretched out in front. "Bad news, I'm afraid," he said. "Those were messengers from the Lisu in Tantsah warning me not to come to town. They say the Chinese authorities have been threatening to seize the houses and property of any Lisu who become Christians. They've really threatened Mr. and Mrs. Tsai. Apparently they think I'm an agent of the British government."

"Even if you were, what crime is that?"

Fraser sighed. "They say I'm here to take away some of their territory for Britain or something. And that Mr. Tsai is my accomplice. It's silly, of course, but, still —"

He shook a stone from his shoe before continuing.

"Anyway, they've scared the Lisu sufficiently that they all signed an agreement not to listen to me or have me live in town."

"What now?"

Fraser shrugged. "We carry on. I still think I should live in Tantsah."

They pulled themselves to their feet and walked on. Jeff's excitement at the destination was suddenly gone. Not only was he stuck with this man he didn't know — a tough, sober, no-nonsense type, whose only interest was this dirty tribe of Lisu — but this eccentric man was going to a remote village of a few hundred people, a village that would provide no way home for Jeff. And, in fact, if that tyrant he'd seen in the first village was any indication of the welcome, they could really be in for trouble.

But until Zeke could bring him back home or he could come up with some better scheme, he had no choice. *Lord,* Jeff prayed silently, *I know I haven't exactly been Your greatest follower, but don't leave me stranded here — please!*

FOUR
Trouble at Tantsah

"We won't make it to Tantsah tonight. Let's camp here and go into town tomorrow."

"Sounds good to me. I'm exhausted."

Immediately Jeff reined the horse, and after helping him dismount, J. O. Fraser unloaded the saddlebags. Ba Thaw dropped to the ground and quickly led the horses to a grassy patch nearby to feed. Jeff helped gather firewood, then watched as his companions built a fire. They put a small pot of water on to boil for tea and steamed rice.

Fraser's saddlebag seemed to hold all he needed. Though Jeff could have wished for more than rice and clear green tea, at least it stopped the gnawing hunger. Besides, they had dessert — berries gathered from nearby bushes.

"I'm going to leave you in the morning," Ba

Thaw said to Fraser as they ate. "I think I'll go off at this point to Turtle Village and on up that valley. You have a traveling companion now anyway." He flashed a big smile at Jeff.

Fraser nodded and grunted his agreement. "Ba Thaw," he said after a minute, "could you lead my horse as far as Turtle Village? I'd like that young widow and her boys there to have it for the next few months. They need it more than I do now. Jeff here can help me carry," and he turned to Jeff for confirmation. "Right?"

"Sure!" Jeff said more enthusiastically than he felt.

"No problem about the horse. Free pasture should be adequate now and improving. Good!" Ba Thaw seemed pleased. Then looking into the distance, narrowing his eyes in thought, he returned to the original subject: "I need to work in a visit to the Kachin and the Shan too, if possible."

"The what?" Jeff asked.

"Tribes," Fraser answered. "All over these hills." Fraser began to roll out his blanket as he talked. He tossed the extra one to Jeff.

"There are several tribal groups in the mountains of China — the Kachin, the Shan, the Wa, the Karen, but the people that really interest me are the Lisu."

"Yeah," Jeff muttered sleepily.

It must have been enough of an answer because Fraser continued: "As far as we know,

before we came, no one had ever spoken to the
Lisu about the love of God. That's why I feel
my particular — well, my assignment from God,
you might say — is to take the Gospel to the
Lisu people. Villages like Mottled Hill, that's the
kind of villages I look for," he said, finding a
comfortable position sitting on the ground.

"That village wasn't too great."

"No, those people are very poor. And dirty.
Filthy, actually."

Jeff was finding it harder than he expected to
get comfortable. His legs ached from the day's
walk, and he was sore all over from horse-back
riding. He wiggled his bones into dips in the ground
under him and tried to relax.

Fraser stared at the stars scattered across the
sky overhead. After a few minutes he said, "I'm
working on making a Lisu script — a way of
writing down the Lisu language."

Jeff yawned. "What d'you mean writing down
the Lisu language? These people have been
speaking it for years — centuries, I guess. Why
don't you learn the writing from them?"

"There's no such thing as written Lisu. They
don't even have any script, any letters to write
with."

Jeff raised up on one elbow. "You mean no
one has ever thought of writing down something
— ever?"

"Never. I started writing down the words just

as they sounded to me. That's why I went to Burma. I've been working with Ba Thaw and some friends there who are experts at this sort of thing, and between us we've made up a script — sort of a standardized alphabet, you might say."

"So are you going to make some books then?"

"Eventually. The Bible, at least. So far we've just put some simple Christian teachings into Lisu."

"Think they can learn to read?"

Fraser nodded. "They're intelligent people. They love to watch me write and ask me what it says. I can teach them to read easily once we get some simple primers written in their language."

"Wow! I never thought of something like that. Making up a whole written language. Hmmm." He studied Fraser, who sat, almost unaware of his companions, staring out at the huge expanse of blackness around them. Tall and muscular, with his long face reflecting the dim starlight and his long, thin hands clasped around his knees, he sat here talking about making up an alphabet for a foreign language as if he were talking about doing a 150-word book report.

Jeff sat up and reached into his jacket pocket and pulled out the piece of paper he had picked up. "I just remembered this. Maybe you know something about it."

Fraser snapped back to attention as he glanced at the paper in Jeff's hand. "Where on earth did you get this?"

"A girl at Mottled Hill Village had it. Doesn't make sense to me. D'you know what it is?"

Fraser grabbed the paper excitedly. "Yes, of course, I know. I wrote it. That's Lisu. That's some of my alphabet I invented. See here this means 'God loves you.'" Fraser was suddenly alive. "Which house were you in?"

"The one nearest the path, on the left. With the big black pig in a pen beside the porch."

"Sure. I know the one. I left this with them on my last visit before I left for Burma. They are one of several families in the area that would believe in Christ if they had more teaching."

Fraser was quiet for a minute, then turned to Jeff and asked, "By the way, Jeffrey, do you know Jesus as Savior?"

"Yes, I accepted Him into my heart when I was quite young."

"That's good, Jeff. Don't hesitate to follow Him wherever He leads you. You won't be sorry."

"Right." Jeff was suddenly glad he was here. Crazy, but he was. Then he remembered the fierce man who had scared him out of his wits at Mottled Hill. "Mr. Fraser," he said, changing the subject back to that first village he visited, "when I was at that house in Mottled Hill, a big guy just stormed in and started yelling at everybody. The people were afraid of him. He didn't like that piece of paper with writing on it a bit. Do you know who he is?"

"Was he wearing a turban and shorts with white leggings?"

"No. Just a padded blue jacket and long pants and no hat. Sort of like the clothes you're wearing. He had shoes, while the others didn't. I think he limped a little."

Ba Thaw sat up and exchanged knowing glances with Fraser. "Oh-oh. You know who that is. No doubt about it."

Fraser nodded. "I'm afraid so." He turned to Jeff. "That's Liang Tingwu. He's the Chinese overlord of the Tantsah district. Sort of a 'warlord,' you might call him. I've heard a lot about that rascal. He's a bad one. Those two messengers who met us back there were telling me that he threw six Lisu men in jail here last week."

"Why? What did they do?"

"Oh, who knows? Happens often. Probably the Chinese 'lord' demanded something the Lisu didn't want to give. Maybe they haven't paid their taxes to him or cut his trees or something. Or maybe a Lisu refused to let the overlord have his daughter to add to his harem. That happens too."

Fraser sat hunched over, knees pulled up under his chin, one arm gesturing. "See," he explained, "all the land is owned by the Chinese. They allow the Lisu to use it quite freely, — live on it, grow gardens and so on — but they demand work in exchange.

"Most of the Chinese overlords are quite reasonable. Oh, the Chinese look down on the Lisu — call them 'earth people' and other not-so-nice names — and the Lisu grumble about having to work for the Chinese, of course; but in general they don't mind too much, and usually there's no trouble. But it depends on the district. A local 'lord' can be very oppressive, if he wants to, and there's very little the Lisu can do. The Chinese have the upper hand."

Jeff nodded. "Sounds like our softball coach. He started yelling at me first game we played, and he never let up. All season, he was on my back. I hated him." Jeff's feelings showed in his voice. "Sounds just like this guy and the Lisu — picking on them for no reason, I mean. I can understand that they hate to see him come around."

Fraser was silent for a while. Then he said thoughtfully, "It all adds up. The incident in the village and now the warning from Tantsah. Liang Tingwu doesn't want us around." He poked at the paper now back in Jeff's hand. "When he saw this paper, he probably thought you had given it to them. So he was telling you, 'Get your honorable skin out of this village, and do not stick your honorable nose in here again,' or some such words!"

"Yeah, it sounded like that! But why blame me?"

Fraser shrugged. "You're a Westerner; they lump us all together. Besides, not many foreign visitors pass through these parts; so he figured you must be one of us."

Jeff shuddered. "Then he won't want me in Tantsah any more than he wants you. I'd just as soon stay out of his way."

"I don't blame you," Fraser answered. "Liang has a reputation as a mean, unfriendly character."

Fraser was silent for several minutes. Finally he drew a deep breath, took a drink of the remaining tea, and turned to Jeff. "Ready to go to sleep?"

Jeff nodded and yawned.

"Right. I always have a time of prayer before I settle in for the night. You're welcome to join me, but don't feel you have to." Then Fraser opened the dog-eared Bible he carried in his bag and read a chapter from Hebrews and then a Psalm, tipping the pages toward the dying fire for light.

Jeff was getting sleepier by the minute, but he felt he should pray when it came his turn. "Dear Heavenly Father," he said quickly, "thank you for helping me today in the village and that I met James and Ba Thaw here. And keep us safe as we travel and especially when we come to Tantsah. Help us not to get into any trouble with that Chinese guy. And give us a good sleep tonight. In Jesus' Name, Amen."

Jeff drifted off to sleep with Fraser and Ba Thaw's voices still praying in the background — for themselves, for the Lisu, for James' family in England, for the situation at Tantsah and the Chinese authorities who were causing the trouble.

It was still early the next morning when Fraser shook Jeff's shoulder and woke him. "We'd better get moving. We've got miles to go. There's a creek a few hundred yards down below there if you want to wash up."

Once Jeff had scrambled back up the bank, his face washed and his hair combed with his fingers, he and J. O. said good-bye to Ba Thaw and the horses and headed down the trail.

The sun had its effect. The mud began to dry, the grass beside the trail pushed up fresh green shoots, and Jeff felt light footed in spite of the bedroll that was now his responsibility. He'd take sunshine over mist and fog any day.

Fraser strode easily on ahead, humming loudly. It was hard to believe this tall, determined man had even heard the warning about Tantsah. He looked totally unconcerned about the danger he was walking into. As much as Jeff was enjoying the hike, he wasn't so sure he was in a hurry to get to Tantsah.

When the road smoothed for a stretch, Fraser slowed his pace and started up conversation as if he suddenly remembered Jeff's presence. "Are you a baseball fan, Jeff?"

"Yeah, sort of. I like soccer and hockey better, when it comes to playing. I play in the local soccer league, and we've got a good ice rink near us where a bunch of us play hockey every Saturday morning during the season. But I like to watch baseball—" he stopped himself just in time. He was going to add "on TV."

"A man after my own heart. You said something about playing the piano. Do you have any other interests?"

In spite of his determination to be on his guard and not arouse suspicions about his "trip," Jeff found himself talking more freely as they walked along. Fraser sounded like he was genuinely interested in him, not just snooping.

"I play the trumpet a bit. And I like biking. We've got a bike group in our church that goes on bike trips together two or three times a year. I have a Schwinn, all-terrain ... a ... a pretty good bike."

He realized Fraser was looking at him oddly. He'd better change the subject. "Tell me about your life in England."

"Not much to tell. I lived a pretty normal life, believe it or not, until I came here," he laughed. "Rather a normal chap, I am."

Jeff smiled in return. *This guy normal?* But to keep him talking, Jeff asked, "What about your family?"

"I have two sisters and three brothers. My father was a veterinary surgeon. In fact, when I was growing up, he was head of the Royal College of Veterinary Surgeons in St. Albans. We lived comfortably then. But, unfortunately, he and my mother separated when I was a teenager."

"My best friend's parents got a divorce last summer," Jeff said, nodding. "He lives just with his mom now."

"Yes, so did we from then on. You'd like my mother — she gave me my love for music and art. I remember when I was about twelve saving up my pennies for months to buy her a bust of Beethoven — you know, a small statue of his head — for her desk."

Fraser bent over to pick a tiny flower that was growing beside the path and stuck it in his button hole, grinning at Jeff as he did so.

"Anyway," Fraser continued, "I ordered this gift, but I didn't know I'd have to wait so long for it to arrive." The energy in his voice kept pace with his steps as he wound in and around bushes and over fallen trees, not missing a word. "Five months! I was nearly beside myself with impatience. I've always been one to get things done, and done now. I nearly broke down and told her about it dozens of times, but I didn't." He smiled at the memory. "Mother still has that bust on her desk," he laughed.

"We used to have some jolly times," the tall missionary continued, his eyes smiling. "I remember we published a newspaper, my brothers and I. Came out once a month. I drew the pictures and lettered — oh, so carefully — a beautiful 'table of contents' on the front cover. We charged for it too — one farthing." He laughed now at the idea. "And we took pictures and sold them to people in the family. Called our make-believe business" — he put on a regal tone — "'The Imperial Photographic Company Limited.' We made up a law that everyone *had* to buy the picture we took of them whether they wanted it or not!" He laughed and tossed a pebble down the mountainside, listening to it hop and skip.

Jeff laughed and told Fraser about his own effort when he was five — the book he'd written about a three-legged chicken named Roosty. "Only I spelled it R-U-S-T-Y," he added laughing. When Fraser was in a talkative mood, it was easy to tell him things.

Before long they saw Tantsah on the hill ahead. It was bigger than the villages Jeff had seen on the trail, but not a lot better. One man, obviously Lisu by his clothes, glanced their way as they approached and slid into the nearest dark doorway. Other Lisu seemed to find business elsewhere till by the time they had entered the village, the street was deserted.

One look at James' face told Jeff what he was

already sure of, that something was very wrong. As they rounded a corner, a man emerged from an alleyway carrying buckets on a shoulder pole. Staggering under his heavy load, he jostled against Fraser's arm, whispered a few terse words and moved on down the street. Fraser gave no indication he had even heard the man.

When they had gone a few yards further, Fraser said quietly without slowing his step, "Don't look around. That was another message. The Lisu don't want me here. They're really afraid. I don't want to make trouble for any of them; so I'll just go in and get my stuff and leave town as quickly and quietly as possible."

The house Fraser called home was a two-room shack no better than the others in town.   Jeff's heart sank. This was the "great little place" he'd talked about? It had nothing, except for a great view and a lot of trees around it. How could James be so thrilled with a place like this? This wasn't what Jeff expected when Fraser said he had a house. Well, it was just as well they weren't staying if this was what he'd have to live in. He wouldn't really feel comfortable, in fact, until they were safely away from the whole village and away from any possible encounter with the angry Liang Tingwu.

"I haven't got much to take; I'll be with you in a few minutes," Fraser called back as he ducked through the doorway.

Obviously Jeff wasn't expected to follow. There seemed to be little room inside for two anyway. So Jeff, for the moment forgetting the danger, strolled around the village while he waited. What a place for a picture! Too bad he didn't put his camera into his pocket instead of his tape player.

Oh, if Mom could only see this! If she were here, she'd get out her sketch pad and start drawing immediately! The whole scene was perfect: tiny, thatch-roofed houses perched on a gigantic mountain, a dusty path for the main street, and everywhere over the hillside fields of corn and other green plants struggling for existence.

There, he thought, *that'd make a good picture.* He strolled toward the only painted building in town, noticing the upturned corners on its roof.

Suddenly the doorway of the gold and red building filled with an overweight man in a dark, loose gown and with a wide, sinister face. As he headed straight for Jeff, shouting and pointing, Jeff recognized the slightly limping gait. *Liang Tingwu!*

Liang Tingwu had recognized Jeff too. The man's eyes flashed anger. Immediately the fat-faced overlord yelled something in Chinese, fingered the sword at his side, and stood right in front of Jeff, blocking his way. Jeff stopped, terrified.

Jeff felt helpless, with Fraser nowhere in sight. His face almost as white as his windbreaker, Jeff smiled weakly, hoping to defuse the man's anger.

With a snap of his fingers the man summoned the skinny, bow-legged servant Jeff had seen before. As if under an order from his boss, the skinny one cracked a whip in Jeff's direction. Jeff ducked. Though he turned to run, it was too late. Liang's fat hand reached out and grabbed him by the shoulder.

"Oww! That hurts!" Jeff protested. "Let go!"

Just then a determined-looking woman ran from the shop where she had been buying corn and hurried over to the scene. She began yelling, apparently standing up to Liang. While Jeff had a passing thought on her bravery, Liang's big fingers were digging into his shoulder too painfully to spare much thought for anybody or anything else.

Now the lady's voice softened into more of a pleading tone. Liang's henchman lashed out at her, the whip grazing her head. She stood her ground. Another man came out of the temple and said something to Liang. Calmed somewhat, Liang lowered his voice a few decibels, but words continued to tumble angrily from his flushed lips. Jeff stood shaking, waiting for what was going to happen next.

From behind him Jeff could hear Fraser's footsteps. James — shedding an awkward load as he moved — ran around to face Liang and his captive, bowed politely and addressed the warlord. Liang Tingwu's fingers loosened their grip, but didn't let go.

Jeff wiggled and squirmed. *Come on, never mind being polite,* he wanted to tell Fraser. *Just belt the guy one and get me out of here! It's all your fault I'm in this mess anyway. I should never have come with you. I should have made my own way. Why did I come to this stupid village anyway?* Jeff was trembling. *Great way to end,* he thought ruefully — *captured by a raving maniac in a tribal village in some remote corner of China! I'll be thrown into a hole in the ground to rot — or who knows what? Oooh, I should never have followed this guy!*

The exchange in Chinese between Liang Tingwu and Fraser was obviously tense. Jeff could see that Fraser was sitting on his temper. By his gestures the towering Britisher was obviously making a point of the fact that he had all his belongings with him and was leaving town. And, yes, he was taking this young trouble-maker with him. He nodded toward Jeff. Liang Tingwu thought for a minute, shouted and pointed again at Jeff, at Fraser, and lastly at the woman who had come to his aid.

Finally, without any warning, the oversized bully released his grip on Jeff's shoulder and stomped off into the building from which he'd come. Jeff stood shaking, too bewildered to move.

"Come on. Let's get out of here," Fraser said brusquely, stuffing the bedding into Jeff's grasp. The missionary's long legs broke almost into a run as he strode out of the village ahead of Jeff. "You just about got us both into deep trouble, young man."

Jeff panted, running to catch up. "Me? Wasn't my fault."

Fraser said nothing. Jeff could see a pulse throbbing in his forehead and his mouth set in rigid lines. He strode on ahead, his few belongings bulging from his backpack.

Jeff had to stop for breath. "Wait a minute! I can't keep up." His breath came hard, hurting his chest. "I didn't do anything."

Fraser slowed his stride only slightly.

"Please. I'm sorry." Jeff panted, slowing to a standstill, the bedroll dangling from a limp arm. "I'm sorry, I didn't mean to get you into trouble."

Fraser slowed and turned to wait for him now.

"I didn't know he would freak out like that," Jeff blurted.

"Well, now you do. Anyway, stay with me. If I'm going to be responsible for you, stay with me. Do you hear?"

Jeff nodded. Responsible for him? This man wasn't responsible for him. He didn't have any right to talk to him like that. Who got him into this mess anyway?

His thoughts churned as he tried to keep up with Fraser's long legs, which were increasing in speed again. He had nothing to say. If this man was going to live dangerously, he didn't need to drag Jeff into it. He had no desire to get himself killed.

The mountains receded into the distance now as the road opened up before them. Gradually Jeff's anger began to subside. Actually it was a good thing Fraser had come to his aid, or who knows what would have happened? And it wasn't really Fraser's fault. It was more like Zeke's. Oh, if only he could get out of here! — out of this decade, out of China, out of the whole mess.

Fraser slowed his steps to accommodate Jeff. They walked on together in silence as the sun dropped low in the west.

"I'm sorry I was angry. I just want to be so careful not to antagonize the Chinese leader for the sake of the Lisu in town. I was hoping to get in and out without trouble. Then you made a scene. That was Mrs. Tsai, by the way, who came to plead your cause. The Chinese already hold Mrs. Tsai and her husband responsible for my activities. Now you probably got her and her family into more trouble." Fraser shook his head in dismay. "But I know, I know ... you couldn't help it."

"Yeah, I'm sorry too. I am glad you rescued me, honest. Look, maybe I'd better leave. You go wherever you're going and I'll go ... somewhere else. If you'll just tell me the direction to a city. Beijing, maybe."

Fraser looked at him, oddly at first, then frowning, and shook his head. "Beijing?" He started to open his mouth but closed it again and changed his expression. "No, indeed. You can't manage on your own in this country. Until you find your parents or come up with some better scheme I'm not going to let you go wandering around by yourself. Like it or not, it looks as if we are stuck with each other."

Well, thought Jeff, *I hope we both survive.*

FIVE

Encounter at the Market

"Where are we headed now?"

"Tengyueh. Big Chinese city on the plateau. The China Inland Mission has a home there, and my friends, the Emberys, live there."

Finally, to Jeff's relief, the trail opened out suddenly, revealing a walled city spread below them.

"There we are. Tengyueh. Be at the Embery's by dark."

A few hours later, as the shadow of the mountains cast long arms over the town, Fraser led the way through a narrow street where vendors were locking up their shops for the night, beyond a brightly painted temple, to a walled compound. Inside the walls, on a paved courtyard, stood a small church. Through a doorway in a nearby building they could see a room with benches for receiving visitors. They walked through this, and entered a door to the living quarters behind it. The house was nearly new, Jeff noticed. It was almost better than he'd dared to hope for after what he'd seen.

No sooner had the travelers made their appearance than a little girl which Jeff judged to be about four raced out of the kitchen to greet J.O., an elderly Chinese lady hurrying behind her. The child ran to Fraser and raised her arms to be picked up.

"Glad to see me again, are you? Have you been a good girl?" Fraser twirled the child around and said a few words of greeting to the servant, whom he introduced to Jeff as Mrs. Li. Still holding the child, he strode on into the living room, Jeff trailing behind him.

"Mrs. Embery, come meet somebody," Fraser called. A stout, motherly-looking woman in a Chinese dress came running downstairs. She gave James a hug. "We missed you. Glad to see you back. Look like you need a good meal." She held out her hand to Jeff, eyes portraying all the questions she refrained from asking. "Hello, I'm Mrs. Embery. Pleased to meet you."

Jeff shook her hand and told his name.

"Where did you come from? How —?" She looked questioningly at James Fraser.

"I met him on the trail. He needs a place to

sleep," was all Fraser said. Jeff could have hugged him right then. Mrs. Embery looked at them both, shook her head, and smiled understandingly. "All right, all right. I won't ask. Honestly, James, I wonder what you're going to do next."

Just then a man's head appeared around the door, and the face broke into a smile. "Well, well, James, you're back, are you? Good to see you again, brother." He shook James' hand vigorously. "Have a good trip, did you?"

Mrs. Embery interrupted. "Here now, you can talk later. Find our friend, Jeffrey, a bed, and then you can both come down and eat."

"Come on upstairs," Fraser said leading the way. "I'll show you where to sleep."

He opened the door to a small, cozy room at the top of the stairs. The window looked out on the town below, where lanterns and candles were beginning to twinkle through cracks in shutters now closing for the night. Jeff sank onto the bed, hardly noticing the straw mattress. He was exhausted. Forget eating; he just wanted to sleep.

"Here, pull this down around you when you go to sleep to keep the mosquitoes from bothering you." Fraser reached for the mosquito net that had been flipped up on top of itself over the bed. "Good night. Nice to be in a real bed again, isn't it? We'll see you in the morning."

Morning brought the smell of bacon wafting

upstairs to Jeff's room. He scrambled out of bed and looked out his window at the tile roofs of the shops around him. The windows and doors that were closed the night before now opened to display fruit, vegetables, cloth, pots and baskets, various wares for sale. Women weighed over nearly double with huge baskets on their backs, jostled in the street against the meat seller bringing in a freshly killed goat, a couple of boys lugging a bucket of water, and right across the street from their gate, a beggar, wailing and turning his head from side to side.

The city was coming to life. It might be fun to go out and snoop around. Lots of things going on that he'd like to have a look at.

He went downstairs following the aroma of breakfast. What he had smelled wasn't really bacon, he discovered, but fat pork. Ugh! Fat pork with rice wasn't his idea of breakfast. Mrs. Embery saw his reaction immediately and assured him he didn't have to eat it. "Just have some of this steamed bread, dear," she told him, pushing a large plate of pale buns toward him. "And here, this fruit's called papaya; you might want a piece of that. Anyone for tea?"

Jeff was just wondering if Fraser were sleeping in when he came through the door, Bible in hand, as if he'd been outside reading for a while. He picked up the Embery's children in turn, giving them a twirl and a kiss on the forehead.

"They're glad to see their 'Uncle' James again," Mrs. Embery said, watching.

While he ate Fraser discussed the events in Tantsah. "The Lisu say if I can get government permission to live in Tantsah, they would still be happy for me to come. I'm glad of that. It seems they're just afraid of the Chinese authorities."

Mr. Embery listened and nodded. "You'd better go somewhere else for a while till things quiet down."

"Yes. I think I should visit these mountains to the southeast." He gave a nod of his head toward the hills visible in the distance. "Hmmm. This tea is so good. Doesn't taste like this boiled in my little tin can, you know."

Mr. Embery passed James' cup to his wife for a refill. "Sounds like the best idea. You haven't been back to some of those villages since you visited them, what — four, five years ago? There may be people ready to believe by now. I think that would be a good plan." He pursed his lips to sip some steaming tea before continuing. "Spend some time in Hsingta, Paoshan, places like that. Splendid idea."

"Aren't there enough people to preach to here in Tengyueh —" Jeff asked, "people that would be glad to listen too?"

"Oh, sure. I do preach here when I'm in town. We have a little congregation here — did you notice the little chapel there as we came in? —

with half a dozen baptized believers, including Mrs. Li, our helper here and our cook. But the Emberys are doing just fine without me.

"Actually I was supposed to come here only to learn Chinese, then go east of here to work with the Lisu in the hills above the city of Sa-pu-shan. The Chinese of Sa-pu-shan are coming to Christ in such large numbers that the two missionaries there can't keep up with them all. Those missionaries, of course, want me to come to help them."

Fraser put another bite of bread in his mouth and continued. "Mr. Hoste — that's our Director — gave me permission to survey the tribes in these mountains around here — just to see how many Lisu there were, where they lived, that sort of thing. I took a little scouting trip and reported what I found — thousands of Lisu villages all over these hills. Well, at first his reply was still, 'Go east where you were sent.'"

"It would have been much easier, mind you," Mr. Embery said, quietly sipping his tea. "The work's going well, the cities are bigger, there's less opposition from the authorities there. But that wasn't for James." He smiled slightly at James, a smile that hardly did justice to the admiration in his eyes.

Fraser cut a piece of bread into quarters before continuing. "I'm not a rebel. I was prepared to do what the directors say. But I just didn't feel that was what I was supposed to do. I didn't refuse. I just prayed about it a while longer."

"Just before I was to leave for the eastern region, Mr. Hoste wrote me another letter; this time he said, 'If you really feel strongly about staying where you are, I won't insist that you go east.'"

"Was he excited then!" Mrs. Embery said quickly. "You went in there and played till I thought the organ would break, so happy you were! Such a concert as we had that night, I tell you."

Fraser said only, matter-of-factly, "So the point is, I'm here for the Lisu — not to stay in a big Chinese town like Tengyueh or Sa-pu-shan. I belong on the mountains."

Fraser finished eating and returned to the living room, where Jeff heard him running his fingers over the keys of the small, portable organ.

"Have some more, love?" Mrs. Embery asked, looking at Jeff. She nodded her head toward the sound. "Beethoven. When James is home, he spends hours at that organ, just playing one piece after another. Sometimes it's Bach, or Chopin. He needs music, you know, just has to have it. It's one thing he misses up on the trails; so we're glad to have him play when he's here."

"He even beats out music in his mind," Jeff said, shoving a piece of the somewhat stodgy Chinese bread into his mouth. "It just runs out of his finger tips."

Mrs. Embery chuckled, a low, resonant chuckle.

"I know, I know. He gives concerts, you know. Full-length piano concerts when he's in Shanghai or any city where there's a piano and enough people to appreciate a touch of Western culture. He was going to be a concert pianist at one time. I don't know which he misses more, his music or his engineering."

"He's an engineer?" Jeff asked, surprised.

"Yes. Would have been if he'd stayed in England. Oh, he'd never tell you all this about himself. He's a talented man, is our James." She lowered her voice to an almost-whisper. "A bit ... unusual sometimes, maybe. Very hard on himself, very self-disciplined. And not one for fooling around, as it were. But brilliant and very gifted. And his Lisu! How he loves his Lisu!"

She said a word or two to Mrs. Li, the old Chinese servant, who seemed to be wanting to clear the breakfast dishes. Then she leaned across the table and looked at Jeff.

"And, you know, it's not that we don't need him here in Tengyueh. He'd be welcome to stay here as long as he wants as far as we're concerned. But that's not James. He gets restless when he's here too long."

Jeff was glad when Fraser agreed to stay a few days. "Even J. O. Fraser, the mountain-goat can't keep walking forever," he said, laughing. After his trek from Burma and the disappointment at Tantsah he seemed really glad of little luxuries like a real bed at night, good food every meal, and the Embery's company — and an organ.

Mrs. Embery took advantage of the extra time Fraser was there. "It'll give me time to work on your clothes, James. If you could see yourself. Pants are too baggy, your jacket sleeves are frayed. Look at this." She shook her head at him, but there was a smile on her face as she did it.

"The way I see it, Mrs. Embery," Fraser said, "when I'm out on the trail, it doesn't matter what I look like because nobody knows me anyway. And when I'm here in town it doesn't matter what I look like because you already know me."

Mrs. Embery let out a mock sigh and then laughed. "And love you. Yes, we do. But you can't go around — Oh, never mind. Just give me that old jacket you're wearing." She went off laughing.

"You know," Fraser said one day as they sat around the table after breakfast, "I've been thinking about something for some time. There are two things the Lisu want to learn, can learn, that will help them — reading and music. Reading is absolutely essential." Mr. Embery was nodding steadily as James went on. "I've maintained that right from the beginning. They can't read God's Word if they're illiterate.

"But music's the other thing," Fraser continued. "You know, it occurred to me that music can be a great teaching tool. If you put parts of

Scripture, for instance, or — well, other facts, Christian teaching, whatever, to music — they could learn it easily as a song. You could teach a lot of truth that way. I've decided I should concentrate more on singing, maybe even give lessons."

Mr. Embery agreed. "I hadn't thought of that, but you've got something there, so you have. Singing lessons. Yes. They'll love it. And they'll remember the teaching better."

"I'm going to try translating one or two songs now to have ready for my next trip."

"Well, can't sit talking any longer. Today is market day," Mr. Embery said, swallowing his last mouthful of tea. He folded his napkin neatly, gave his wife a circumspect peck on the forehead, and pushed himself away from the table. "We usually go out on market day and hand out literature and so on. Why don't you come along with us, Jeffrey, and see what a good Chinese market's like?"

Jeff agreed. After all, he couldn't stay in the house the whole time he was here. Anyhow it'd be kind of fun to see what was going on. Putting on a jacket he borrowed from Mr. Embery, which was a little shorter than the one he'd worn on the trail, he followed his two seniors out to the street.

The city was surrounded by a wide wall on which people strolled or did exercises. The market was set up under a roof, each tiny space selling a variety of wares. Jeff could identify some of it: greens like his mother used to make, Chinese vegetables, bulbs of garlic, long cucumbers, bright red peppers and a type of cooking banana, also things like salt, honey, and tea. Other merchants were selling bolts of dark blue cloth, Chinese shirts and gowns, tortoise-shell combs, and imported products like condensed milk.

In the distance rose a pagoda and to the left of that a large building, surrounded by a high wall. All Jeff could see over the wall was the elaborate tiled roof.

"That's the *yamen*, the home of the Chinese district overlord," Embery explained. "Quite a lavish place, really."

"You mean the one that's causing so much trouble for the Lisu around Tantsah? That — what's his name? — Liang something?"

"That's the one. That's his official residence, though he has several."

"Big place, isn't it? It'd be neat to go in and see inside the wall."

"I've been in. Yes, it's very big. And luxurious. Lots of servants running around all over the place. Very impressive."

Hmmm, Jeff thought. *No wonder the Lisu were afraid.*

As Jeff watched, Mr. Embery handed out literature to anyone who was willing to take it.

"What's that you're giving out?" he asked.

"This one's just a simple explanation of who Jesus Christ is; this one explains the way to Heaven like a bridge across a great gulf. The death of Christ is the bridge that makes it possible for people to cross the big canyon. It's based on a preaching poster we use."   Then Jeff remembered where he'd seen it before. One of the Chinese Christians used to preach from that poster in Taylor's clinic in Hangzhou! "This little book is the Gospel of Mark," Mr. Embery continued. "Of course, we only have it in Chinese, but as soon as he can James is going to translate it into Lisu."

Two or three Lisu visitors followed them back to the mission home. Mrs. Embery looked at each one in turn, noticing the rough blotches all over their arms and legs.

"Oh, he's got such a skin rash, he has," she said of one boy. "Rashes — very common among the Lisu. I give them this." She led the way to the supply room, stocked with literature on one side, medicine on the other. Jeff watched her pick out the appropriate bottle from the small supply and return to the visitors, who seemed delighted with their treatment.   Maybe if he learned where things were, he could help give out medicines like he used to do for Hudson Taylor. His parents would never believe all the things he had done in Taylor's clinic — things his father would never do in his practice in Rochester.   But they'd saved lives. Even simple medicines were better than nothing.

Over and over the scene was repeated daily as Lisu and individuals from other tribes came to the mission house for care. No one left without literature if he could read and medicine if he needed it.

Once he was familiar with the market, Jeff found himself enjoying a walk through the haphazard spread of stalls under the long, sometimes sagging roof. Some of the food smelled delicious. And it was always interesting to watch the different hill-people come in on market day with their distinctive costumes and with their wares for sale. Jeff soon learned to identify the Lisu and the Kachin and even picked up a few phrases of Chinese as well as a Lisu word or two.

He stopped to look at a stall of wooden toys. The man at the next counter was bargaining for some tea, a product the Lisu didn't have unless they bought it from the Chinese. As Jeff watched, the girl by the man's side spotted Jeff and grabbed her father's sleeve. In a moment, getting no response, she broke away from her father and ran over to Jeff, grinning broadly.

Jeff remembered now. It was the girl that had welcomed him at the first house he had visited that day he'd landed in the rain and needed help. The one he'd called Jingles. Her hair was longer now and he didn't recognize her at first.

That had been several weeks ago, and she seemed to have gotten even dirtier in the meantime. She had a runny nose and scabs covered her arms and neck. Jeff shuddered. How could a kid ever get to look this bad? He didn't want to touch her. He smiled at her and moved a few steps back. She stood staring at him openly, taking in all the details of his face and clothing.

Her father saw her now and came over to join them. He was grinning and bowing all the while. The father seemed to be telling him something significant, but Jeff didn't understand a word. He smiled, nodded and looked generally interested. He'd have to learn some Lisu if he was going to stay here longer. This was stupid, to be able to say nothing. Wait, he was getting the picture. The man kept pointing to his child's scabs and saying the same words over and over, whatever they were. Then he pointed out a bad ulcerated area on his own leg and repeated the word. He must be asking for some medicine or treatment for all these skin sores.

"I can't understand you," Jeff said loudly and slowly. "I don't know what you mean." Well, never mind words. He waved his arm for them to follow and began to walk out of the market area. They followed quickly, afraid to lose him in this unfamiliar place as he wound his way along the streets toward the mission house.

Inside the gate he called for Mrs. Embery. She

could understand them and would know what to do. She talked to the father and girl several minutes before turning to Jeff with an explanation.

"Her name is Nyio-sa-mei." To Jeff it sounded something like New-saw-may. "And of course, since she's the oldest child," Mrs. Embery was saying, "her father is called by her name, with the syllable 'pa' stuck on the end. So his name is Nyio-sa-mei-pa."

"What about her mother?" Jeff asked, grinning, "I suppose her name is Nyio-sa-mei-_ma_?"

"Exactly. You catch on quickly."

"Is it really?" Jeff laughed. "I was only kidding. I didn't expect it to work that way. Are all the Lisu named for their children? What a funny idea!" _So Mum and Dad would be Jeff-pa and Jeff-ma if they did this at home!_ Jeff smiled at the thought.

"Yes, that's the way they do it. They're Flowery Lisu — see their pretty colored clothes." Mrs. Embery touched Nyio-sa-mei's blue apron with the red and white patches on it and the jingly cowry shells along the hem. She smiled at the dirty girl and said something in Chinese. "The Black Lisu wear only navy blue clothes." She said a bit more to the man who answered, pointing and smiling.

"He says they're from Mottled Hill Village, over that way. She took the girl's thin arm and bent back her head to let light shine on Nyio-sa-mei's dirty face.

"Oh, dear, more of these skin conditions; we see so much of that. It's all caused by dirt. Just good hygiene habits would solve so many of their problems." She went to the cupboard for the small box of medicines. Jeff watched as she mixed a small amount from a bottle labeled "Sulfa Powder" with some kind of grease.

"What are you doing that for?"

"This makes a sulfa ointment for them that will eventually clear up the condition if they use it regularly. We don't have anything else."

Well, it'd better work, thought Jeff. *It smells awful.*

"And the child has a runny nose. Seems perpetual. The kids always have colds and coughs. They don't have proper warm clothing for the cold weather they get up on the hills."

She wrapped a couple of tablets in paper and gave them to the father with instructions. "In the rainy season, they get so much diarrhea. Babies often die of it. I think the colds that plague them this time of year are at least easier to treat."

"He should use this salve three times a day until the skin clears up," she said. "And he needs to take these pills for the big ulcer on his leg. Ointment won't be enough."

"Looks like some penicillin would do the trick," Jeff said.

"Some what?"

"Oh, nothing. I guess you don't have any."

He was going to add "yet" but caught himself in time.

Jeff went to the cupboard where the literature was kept. He knew Fraser would want these Lisu to have some before they left. Even though they probably couldn't read Chinese, they could get somebody to read the characters to them. Fortunately the stacks on the shelves were labeled in English; so he didn't have to guess. Hmmm. He chose a tract called "The Human Heart" and a small paperback copy of the Gospel of Mark and handed them to the father.

When the Lisu were ready to leave, Jeff walked with them to the door and out the gate to the street. The father tucked his medicine and the literature in the folds of his clothes. Both father and daughter smiled and bowed, and Jeff folded his hands and said, "Thank you," over and over because it was one of the few words he knew in Chinese, and it seemed like the thing to do. Happy with the results of the day's business, the Lisu walked on down the street.

The Lisu were friendly people — there was no question about that. They'd probably read the literature too, or rather find someone that could read it to them, and then pass it on. It would get good use. Surely the Lisu could learn to read for themselves if someone taught them, though Chinese characters, he had to admit, looked almost impossible to learn. There were so many of them

— a different character, Mr. Taylor had once told him, for every word! No wonder very few Lisu could read Chinese!

Jeff stuck both hands in his jacket pockets as he walked. He wished he could put on his headphones and hear a good tape right now. But as usual, he had left his tape player at the house hidden under his pillow. He didn't want to have to explain it to James Fraser or the Emberys. And he certainly wouldn't want it stolen. He hummed the phrases he had heard Cray sing so often. "River. Ri-i-ver. Don't I wish you'd flow ____"

Suddenly he sensed a figure standing only inches in front of him, staring at him. He looked up slowly, following the Chinese shoes, baggy pants and wadded gown with side buttons to a fierce face. His breath stuck in his throat. *It was Liang Tingwu!*

SIX

Mad Man, Mad Dogs

Liang Tingwu stood with his fat feet apart, defi-
ance written all over his face. He said something
to Jeff, barking, face red with rage.

Jeff stopped, mouth suddenly dry, knees shaking. He forced himself to stand still and return
the man's gaze. "I don't understand you," he said,
loudly.

Just looking at Liang was enough to make Jeff
shudder. The man looked crabby with his wide,
flat face so flushed with anger. "Crab-face" —
that was a good name for him.

The magistrate pointed off in the direction of
the two Lisu, shouting something about them.

"You don't want us to help them, right? Why?
You are a bully, d'you know that?"

The man's eyes blazed. Seeing he was getting

nowhere with this insolent foreign boy, he strode past Jeff and hurried to catch up with the Lisu, who were wandering slowly, looking at the stalls as they made their way out of town. In a few strides he had caught up with them.

Jeff boiled. He probably should run while he had the chance. But he couldn't just go off and let Liang treat these people like dirt. He turned and followed the Chinese magistrate through the crowd.

The man shouted something, and the Lisu man quickly pulled out the ointment and papers he had just received.

Curiously the Chinese opened the jar and sniffed the medicine. He put his finger in and pulled out a daub and put it in his mouth. Immediately, his face wrinkled up in distaste. He spat on the ground, over and over. Disgustedly, he flung the jar to the ground. Then he took the papers from the man's hand, glanced at them briefly, shredded both the Gospel of Mark and the "Human Heart" tract and sent the bits fluttering in the wind.

Before he could think what he was getting into, Jeff stepped forward. "No, no. You can't do that. I don't care who you are." He was getting really mad now. "You have no right to terrorize everybody. They didn't do you any harm — you leave them alone." He bent over and retrieved the remains of the literature.

The man knocked the paper from Jeff's hands and began shouting at him again. Shaken, the two mountain people bent quickly to pick up the bits of paper and the medicine, and ran toward the path to their village.

Liang flashed a menacing glance at Jeff, saying something else in a demanding voice, then, just as suddenly as he'd appeared, he stormed off. Jeff watched him go. His legs suddenly began to wobble. Only now did he realize how close he had come to trouble.

It was early February, and though the mountains would be even colder than the plains were and more miserable than when they came, Fraser was eager to get going again. "I'll head south, looking for Lisu. And I think you, Jeff, should come with me."

Jeff gulped. "Me? I don't know — I'm not anxious to go on another hike with you. It's easier living here."

"I know. But I need a companion. Just ask Mrs. Embery here. I need someone to make up for all my idiosyncrasies and keep me sane, right?"

Mrs. Embery laughed. "Well I wouldn't say that. But you do need the company all right. Maybe you'll eat properly and look after yourself better if you have someone with you. Jeff would be able to help you with a lot of things."

Jeff thought for a minute. He wasn't eager for

another run-in with Liang. Besides, though the Emberys were friendly and more than willing to give a home to anyone needing it, they hadn't actually asked for his company, and James had. Maybe he could really be of some help.

"Okay, I guess I'll go. Anyway, I don't want to stay here with Liang sneaking around. Count me in."

From the way Fraser described it they'd be just east of the mist-veiled mountain range that Jeff had seen in the distance as they walked into town. After supper the night before their departure Fraser walked out to a quiet place he had discovered where he could pray.

"He won't be back for hours," Mrs. Embery told Jeff. "You might as well go to bed." Jeff awakened later as Fraser came upstairs to bed long after the house was quiet.

By dawn the next morning, a banging on the gate awakened the household. Who could it be at this hour?

Jeff jumped out of bed and looked out the window. Sure enough, there was James, not only up, but dressed, packed and eager to get going. He was talking to a man Jeff decided must be Ah-Do, the man who was to accompany them. One of Mrs. Tsai's sons from Six Family Hollow, Ah-Do was going to be guide, carrier and traveling companion on this trip.

There was little to take. Besides the bedroll

Jeff himself had nothing but his jacket and a small bundle of clothes Mrs. Embery had found for him. He zipped his recorder safely inside an inner pocket. James Fraser took only his Bible, a bag of literature, a change of clothing, a package of food, and a couple of pots, one for boiling water and another for cooking rice.

Ah-Do shouldered Fraser's heaviest pack, then reached over and relieved Jeff of the bedroll, and they were off. It was cold, and at times the wet rocks froze over, making walking hazardous. They hadn't walked many hours before Jeff was thoroughly wet, legs aching, feet tired, shins scratched from slipping on a rocky face.

James seemed impervious to the circumstances. He climbed on and on, reveling in every foot of altitude gained. Even the cold and ever-menacing mist didn't seem to touch him.

"Well, we'd better stop for the night as soon as we come to a good spot," he said finally. Jeff was overjoyed. "It'll soon be dark, and we need a meal anyway."

"I'll second that," Jeff agreed.

Jeff thought he'd fall asleep immediately. He was exhausted, his legs and feet were ready to give up their job for the day, and with the fire smoldering he was warm enough inside the bedroll Fraser had brought for him. But for some reason going to sleep wasn't as easy as he expected. Even banked for a long slow burn as it was, the fire still sent occasional sparks skyward and crackled and popped from time to time. Mosquitoes plagued them, and the light drizzle continued all night. Finally Jeff drifted off, head pulled into the bedroll so that only his hair stuck out. Not much food for mosquitoes in that, so maybe now they'll leave him alone.

By the time he awoke it was morning.

The rain increased as the morning wore on. Soon they were slogging through mud almost up to their ankles.

"Yuck! My feet are all covered in this stuff," Jeff complained. "I can hardly pick my foot up; it's all caked in this muck. Oh, brother, what a trip!"

"I know, it's no fun. I prefer to travel in the dry season whenever possible, and this is one good reason. But, think of it this way, at least it's clean mud, not like the filthy, slimy, dark green stuff around pig pens and cattle sheds that we'll find in some of the villages."

"Thanks a lot," Jeff groaned. "That doesn't help any. Hey! Help!" Before Jeff realized it, both feet were stuck tight in ooze. He pulled at first one foot then the other, and the more he struggled, the more he slipped in. He could feel a steady suction pulling his legs under. In moments mud was licking mid-way up his calf. "I'm sinking. Help!"

Ah-Do shouted something to Fraser and began

hauling a dead branch from nearby bushes.

While Ah-Do dragged the branch to the mud-hole, Fraser stretched to grab Jeff's hand. "Hang on, boy! Don't worry, we'll get you out. This happened to me once. Ah-Do knows what to do."

The men were exchanging comments now. With one hand Fraser helped Ah-Do lay the large branch across the mud, so that both ends rested on solid ground.

"Hold onto this and try to climb up onto it," Fraser commanded.

Jeff grabbed the branch and threw himself over it, feet still trapped in mud. Though it sagged beneath his weight, it held. Slowly he pulled on one foot, then the other, until they were free. He drew his legs up and turned so that he was lying on the tree branch, only a few inches above the mudhole.

With Fraser encouraging him, a trembling Jeff crawled slowly, inch by inch, clinging to the narrow branch, pulling himself along on his stomach. Gradually he reached the end and was able to pull his feet out onto solid ground.

"Whew!" he wiped the rain off his face with his arm. He had forgotten about the drops falling on him in his concern over being stuck. "Thanks." He panted and leaned back against a rock face for support. "Thank you. That was scary there for a minute!"

"Right. As I said, when something like that

happened to me a while ago, I was literally in quicksand up to my neck. Ah-Do, here, and a couple other Lisu friends lay flat on the mud and moved — sort of like swimming — out to reach me." He laughed now at the memory. "We probably looked pretty funny, but we didn't think about it then! I was just glad to be out of there alive. I know how you feel."

Fraser opened the little shoulder bag he had with him. "Here, let's stop and have a snack. It'll make you feel better before we carry on."

Jeff looked on in amazement as J. O. Fraser reached into his pack and pulled out a package of raisins and a little bag of cookies made fresh by the cook just before they left Tengyueh. Jeff had not seen any food like that around the place. He didn't think Fraser ever ate such delicacies!

"Wow, thanks! I didn't know you could get stuff like this here."

"You can buy a lot of things in the market, but most of the time we try to live like the Lisu live, and since they can't afford luxuries like this, we avoid buying them too. But you're not used to traipsing around these peaks all day and eating only rice and greens like I am. I thought you might like something a little more like home."

"Thank you very much." Jeff said softly, helping himself. "Don't you ever get tired of Lisu food?"

"Sure I do. I dream of good old fish and chips,

golden and crisp. Or plum pudding. My mother used to make the best plum pudding you ever tasted. Mmmm, I can taste it now."

"My mom's a great cook too. My friends all like to come to my place 'cause they know they'll get good food. Brownies. And chocolate chip cookies ... and lots of things." The perplexed look had crossed James' face again. So Jeff steered to safer ground. "Maybe you could get your mum to send you some stuff sometime."

"No, it would take so long to get here it would be spoiled. Mind you, she does send me magazines and things other than food from time to time. She knows what I'd like.

Mother and I are a lot alike. We are, in fact, a team. Since I've been in China she has gathered a group of friends who meet every week in her living room there in Letchworth to pray for me. It takes months, of course, for them to get a letter from me; so the news is old by the time they get it, but they keep on praying anyway." Here he stopped and looked at Jeff, "I honestly do not know what I'd do without that group. Their prayers keep me going."

Jeff trudged on behind Ah-Do, who was leading them slowing along a rocky ledge again.

The roar of water reached their ears before they saw the sight. An otherwise harmless stream had been swollen with rain and turned into a rushing torrent. Through the little valley, it rushed along, swirling and sweeping branches, small shrubs, anything that floats along with it.

"Do we have to cross that?" he asked, turning to Fraser.

"Yes. I'm afraid so. We have to go across and up that mountain on the other side."

They stopped by the water's edge to confer. Ah-Do looked around.

"He says there are not enough bamboo trees here to make a proper raft," Fraser translated. More discussion. Ah-Do was cutting one extra-large bamboo now. Chopping it into two pieces about six feet long each, he strapped them together with narrow bamboo strips.

"There —" Fraser said, smiling, "there's our bridge. More like a floating walkway. But it may not take us all at once. Here, let Ah-Do pole you across first and then come back for me."

Jeff looked at Fraser, then at Ah-Do.

"Will it hold? Won't sink, will it?"

Fraser shook his head. "Oh no, it'll float. That's not the problem."

Jeff stepped cautiously onto the two-pole raft, and Ah-Do eased himself on behind him, shoving them off with the long, slender bamboo pole in his hand. Jeff soon saw what the problem was. Trying to stand on wet bamboo only a few inches wide was more of a challenge than he thought. And there was nothing to hold on to. And when Ah-Do got on, the raft sank slightly, holding steady about six inches below the water. "There I go again, up to my ankles in water," Jeff said. But it held and moved gradually downstream at the command of Ah-Do's pole.

As cold as the water was, Jeff sat down to avoid falling off. His teeth chattering, he talked himself into calmness as the little platform floated towards the other shore. As they hit rough water nearing the far side, all of a sudden the makeshift craft was tossed up at one end and twirled around in a sweeping eddy. Jeff grabbed the sides of the raft and lay flat on his stomach. Now he was completely wet. Only inches from his head were rocks protruding from the bank. A log also moved by on his left. Jeff didn't know if he scream-ed or not — not that it would have mattered. Nothing could be done anyway.

Between sprays Jeff opened his eyes to get a glimpse of Ah-Do's sinewy brown legs flexing and tensing as he fought to keep his balance. Skillfully he used his pole to ease them slowly, surely away from the rough water, toward a land-ing place. Finally, with one final push, he shoved the little platform up onto the shore, and Jeff crawled off, dripping and shivering. He flopped on the ground and lay there limply while the bamboo raft made its way back for James Fraser. What a ride!

Even James seemed a little shaken when he was safely across. "Well, we can thank the Lord for His help in that one. This is rough water."

Jeff said nothing. He hadn't thought of it as something to be thankful for. He could sure think of a lot *not* to be thankful for. He was wet and cold for a start. And his legs hurt, and his head ached. He — but Fraser was praying now. "And we thank Thee, Heavenly Father, for getting us all safely across the water. We thank Thee for Ah-Do's company and help on this trip. Now be with us, we pray, as we continue."

Well, that was one way of looking at it. Just like Hudson Taylor and Maria, no matter how bad things got they could always find something to thank God for. Unbelievable, except that Taylor, Maria, James, all of them, weren't unbelievable when you knew them.

Jeff suddenly looked at James, who was rubbing a bad scrape on his shin. Here he was, hurt and wet too, this man who was a trained engineer and who could have been a concert pianist. It was incredible. Jeff shivered. How could he complain? And he was alive, wasn't he? He at least had that to be glad for.

Up the narrow path on this side of the mountain they wound, clothes drying gradually as they walked. Jeff heard James' deep voice humming as he strode ahead. Now and then he burst into full song. Jeff struggled to keep up.

As the afternoon wore on, the sun tried to break through the mist with occasional success.

"Are these mountains always covered in this fog?"

"When the sun shines, the mist rolls off sometimes to show you the whole peak," James called back over his shoulder. "But even then, there's often mist up above five or six thousand feet. Sort of low hanging clouds."

Jeff shivered. If they could just get out of the damp mist that clung everywhere, he'd feel a lot better about this trip. Something about this shadowy atmosphere made him uneasy.

They were reaching a village now, ramshackle huts hugging the hillside some distance ahead. Good. Maybe they'd stop and get a meal and a rest.

The sound of barking dogs met them as they approached. Fraser slowed his pace to talk to Jeff. "Almost every village has their pack of wild dogs as protection against invaders. They're more effective than any city wall, I tell you. Sounds like this one's no exception. Just be careful, and don't make any hasty moves."

Before they reached the village, a fierce-looking cur darted out to meet them, two others right behind him. Their barking summoned all their troops and within minutes a pack of wild, snarling beasts surrounded them.

"Look out!" Fraser shouted over his shoulder.

Their gaping mouths dripped with saliva. Fangs bared, upper lip curled, they ran toward James, growling and eager.

At the moment the dogs seemed not to see Jeff or Ah-Do; they were intent on James. Jeff backed up slowly, climbing up onto a large rock. The dogs could easily reach him, as his perch was only three or four feet high; but he felt a little safer from this vantage point. Jeff watched, heart trying to beat its way out of his chest.

As if a dog bite weren't enough in itself, Jeff couldn't help worry about rabies. They didn't need that on top of everything else. *Rabies — is there any cure for it yet?* he wondered. *In 1915? Yes, there should be, but probably not away up here.* He stood stock still, hardly daring to breathe.

As the dogs circled James, he waved his arms and shouted something in Chinese but to no avail. The last one joined the pack, and they stood growling, snarling, gaping, as if unsure who should attack first.

It took only a second, however, for the most aggressive to make his move. Running for James' right leg, he grabbed for his calf. In no time the others had joined him. Then it all happened in an instant. Suddenly, Fraser was down on the ground, covered with the biting, snapping, half-starved creatures.

Ah-Do picked up a stick and ran towards the melee, waving his weapon wildly and shouting. Jeff forgot his fear. He jumped from the rock on which he was standing and picked up a big branch. Following Ah-Do's example, he ran to the dogs, yelling and flailing the stick.

Ah-Do was hitting furiously at one dog, then another. Jeff joined in. Whacking and swinging, he attacked the two still holding on to Fraser's leg. With all his might he lowered the branch across the shoulders of the more timid one. *Whomp!* With a loud yelp and a trailing whimper, the animal took off. But, where his tooth had punctured Fraser's leg, blood oozed. The other dog held on, his eyes wild. Jeff swung the stick for all he was worth. With a forceful blow he hit the cur on the head. The animal released his hold on James, turned around and ran off yelping after the first one. Intimidated, the other dogs joined it, running, howling, tails between their legs, making for the hills.

With Ah-Do trembling beside him, Jeff bent over Fraser, who lay, shaking and groaning on the ground. Out here in the middle of nowhere, with James so hurt, what would they do?

SEVEN
Excitement of Different Sorts

"What'll we do? We've got to get some help for you," Jeff fretted. Fraser was a mess. From his cheekbone to his ankle teethmarks, some of them trailing blood, tatooed his body. From where a piece of flesh had been gouged out on his right leg blood flowed in a jagged stream, reddening the ground.

Ah-Do and Jeff put Fraser's arms across their shoulders and helped him stand. The wounded man winced as he stood on his left foot and gingerly put weight on the right one. "I think I can walk to the village," he said, his voice weak and husky, "if you both help me."

Slowly they inched their way forward, trying to minimize the jolts and bumps. Fraser limped on painfully, his teeth clamped to ease the pain.

Ah-Do and Jeff encouraged him with every step. Blood by this time was oozing down Fraser's leg into his shoe.

By the time the trio hobbled within shouting distance of the village, dozens of pairs of eyes followed their movements. "We've come in peace," Ah-Do shouted, acting as spokesman, "The foreigners bring good news."

In spite of their untamed dogs, the people seemed not unfriendly — nervous, perhaps, but not unfriendly. Apologetically the man of the house nearest the trail welcomed the strangers inside. Many villagers crowded in after them.

The house was like the one Jeff had seen before, only this one had a little mound of dirt with a cast iron box thing in it over the fire to form a stove. These folks must be wealthier, Jeff decided. They had a few more baskets and bags around too.

The host stoked up the fire, which was already producing enough smoke for two fires.

Fraser reached in his shoulder bag for the tiny supply of medicines he carried.

"You don't have any bandages," Jeff told him, sorting through the pack Ah-Do was carrying. "You've gotta get a bandage on that one leg, especially. Let me see —" Fraser pulled up his pantleg. Fresh blood was trickling bright red over older, darkened blood.

Jeff pulled off his T-shirt which he had been

wearing under his Chinese jacket. He felt conspicuously white. But before putting his T-shirt back on, he tore off the bottom six inches with help from Fraser's penknife. The shirttail was yellow, not white, and certainly not bandage material. But it was all they had. He held it in front of the fire till it steamed dry, hoping that the steaming would sterilize it somewhat.

Carefully Jeff wrapped the soft rag around Fraser's leg, securing the makeshift bandage with a safety pin. Wouldn't stay on very long, probably, but it was the best he could do.

Soon, the three travelers were steaming and sizzling, warm again for the first time all day. The hostess, silver jewelry jangling as she worked, ladled rice into bowls, topped it with greens, added a bit of ground red pepper, and watched, smiling, as they all ate. It tasted a lot better than the last time he ate tribal food, Jeff noticed.

When they'd eaten, Fraser leaned forward, elbows on his knees, watching the fire, and Jeff could see him relax for the first time all day.

Fraser winced, though, when he shifted to face his host, who wanted to know what the good news was they brought.

"There is a God stronger than all other powers. He's the One who created the world, the sun, the stars, the moon — everything." It was obvious that Fraser was distracted by pain and light-headedness. But he went on, "The good news is that He loves you." He dropped his head and closed his eyes, obviously struggling.

Ah-Do stepped in. "This God loves us so much that He sent His own Son to be a sacrifice." He hesitated. Fraser urged him on with a nod. "It means He doesn't want to be angry with us for the things that we do He doesn't like." Used to the idea of trying to make the spirits happy with sacrifices, his audience got the point.

Jeff felt totally left out as questions and answers ping-ponged between Ah-Do and various Lisu men, who were sitting on their haunches, their faces reflecting the flickering of smoky pitch torches. But he was encouraged by the brightness of James' eyes, though his face was gray with pain.

The host took it for granted that his guests would stay the night. Jeff was appalled at how dirty the floor was, but rolled up his change of clothes under his head, pulled his blanket over him, and was soon asleep. James shifted uncomfortably beside him, sleeping little.

"We've had our share of adventure on this trip so far, haven't we?" Fraser commented the next morning as they snail-paced their way along the uneven trail. Ah-Do led the way with Fraser's load added to his own.

"Are all your trips like this?" Jeff asked the hobbling Fraser just ahead of him.

"Well not quite. But they usually have their

dangerous moments. Plenty of them. I'm often attacked by dogs, though not usually this badly. I've been shot at and robbed." He ran one hand over the wounded leg, noticing the blood still oozing through the bandage. He smiled faintly at Jeff and continued, trying to sound light and breezy. "What good's a trip without some adventure?"

"Adventure? Getting yourself half-killed, you mean. I can't see why you do it."

"Last night was worth it, don't you think?" he smiled and thought a minute. "But, well, to tell you the truth, sometimes I wonder myself why I keep on here in these wilds. I'm not crazy — I don't really enjoy suffering. Sometimes I'd rather be home in my mother's kitchen smelling a steak-and-kidney pie baking in the oven."

"Yeah, and warm and dry," Jeff added, wishing the haze would lift and let the sun shine.

"Yes, warm and dry. Safe. Comfortable. Not chewed upon by dogs." He winced as the trail forced him to take a high step. Letting out a loud breath and leaning momentarily against a tree, he continued: "But, no, I wouldn't really change places. Oh, I dream about it at times like this — but if I had to do it again, I'd make the same decisions." He retrieved a rough pole from the bushes, leaning on it as he continued down the path. "Someday there will be churches all over these mountains, churches of Lisu Christians. That's my goal. That's why I do it."

Jeff didn't have an answer. Sure, it sounded noble. And, as unlikely as it seemed now, maybe there really would be Lisu Christians here someday. But wasn't there an easier way to get the job done? He wasn't sure it was worth this.

James' wounds healed gradually as they traveled. He didn't seem as worried about rabies as Jeff was. *Of course, if there's nothing we can do about it anyway, I guess it's just as well not to waste time worrying about it,* Jeff thought.

Fraser was in good condition, no doubt of that. He limped a little when his leg hurt him, but before many days he was marching along with long, confident strides over ridge after ridge.

"New territory, Jeff, all new. I've never been in these villages before. Who knows how many Lisu there are around here? Maybe some that want to believe in Christ."

Ah-Do — young despite his name, which meant "Old Five," Fraser explained — had proved invaluable on the trip. And not only carrying. From that night he first opened his mouth, he had grown increasingly bold in explaining God's way as they stopped in village after village. Fraser was sad when the day came they had to say goodbye to this budding evangelist.

Jeff and James had walked all day that fourth day after Ah-Do had returned to his family. Jeff was developing muscles he never knew he had and was every bit as good a walker as Fraser now. But they were both tired by the time the sun shed its last rays over the hills and highlighted the obviously Chinese town in the valley below.

"We'll stop here," announced Fraser. "Hsingta, I think this town is called."

The next morning Jeff put on a shirt Mrs. Embery had sent with him and combed his hair with a comb she had rustled up from somewhere. "Are we going to look around the town today?" Jeff asked eagerly. "Looks like a pretty good-sized town, compared to some. Let's see if they have some decent food."

"Later, Jeff. We'll visit the town later. After we eat something out of our pack I have to find some place away from the crowd where I can be with God for a few hours. I just feel I need it. If God doesn't bless what I do, there's no sense being here."

Jeff sighed and said nothing. He was used to seeing this by now. For all his energy and love for work, Fraser seemed to spend more time reading the Bible and praying than anyone he'd ever known. While Fraser sat on a gentle slope overlooking the countryside reading and praying, Jeff tried not to get bored. He roamed the hillside, found a bat-filled cave, picked some berries and rested. It was good to sit for a while. He even did a little praying himself.

Finally late in the afternoon Fraser was ready.

"Let's go. I feel much better. Let's see if we can find what you call 'decent food.'"

"Wow, what's going on? Look at the crowd over there!"

A troop of actors belonging to a theatrical company, dressed in bright, noticeable costumes, occupied the central square of town and seemed to be setting up for a play. The crowd was gathering expectantly; the play hadn't yet begun.

Fraser brought out the tiny accordion he carried, moved to the center of the crowd and began to sing. His voice was smooth and melodious, even though Jeff knew he was tired. He recognized the tunes James was singing — tunes of hymns with Chinese words, or sometimes Lisu words. When he finished four or five hymns, he began to preach, using the posters he carried to explain the way of salvation from sin and fear.

A hoot came from the back, and Jeff was aware of some loud talking and laughing. But gradually the troublemakers wandered off, and a hundred people or more stood around the tall foreigner listening to his message. The crowd stood in silence, listening to news they had never heard.

"Would anyone like to know more about Jesus Christ, the Savior of the world?" James asked finally, when he saw that the drama group was ready to begin.

"Yes, I would." A man, about thirty years old,

was stepping out from the people and approaching James. Jeff understood enough to know he was eager to hear the message. They left the square to the theater company and together walked briskly through the streets to the man's house. He led them upstairs to his living quarters over the shop, and there he had them be seated. Jeff was surprised to see how eager this man was to talk to Fraser.

"He says his name's Moh Tingchang," Fraser told Jeff. "He's a chef, a baker." Besides three wooden-plank beds, the large room where they sat was piled with such things as bales of cotton, baskets and bins, piles of firewood, and big earthenware jars. Now the inquirer was digging in a small box — *like a kid looking in a treasure box,* Jeff thought. The man pulled out a book and rushed over to show James. He was talking quickly now with a long explanation of some sort.

When Moh Tingchang finished, Fraser explained to Jeff: "This is a copy of the Gospel of Mark in Chinese." His eyes showed the wonder of the story he was passing along. "It's quite amazing, really. He says his son brought it back from the market in Mangshi, a town just south of Paoshan, five years ago when I was visiting there. I remember the incident.

"I was giving out literature one day, and everybody was pushing and shoving to get in closer, the way they always do. All of a sudden someone knocked my table over — I don't know if it was intentional or an accident. Anyway, the books were scattered everywhere. And while I gathered them up, people helped themselves. I couldn't keep an eye on everyone at once. Well, it seems his son, who was only six or seven at the time, stuck one of the little Gospels in his shirt and ran home with it because he knew his father would like it. This is it! He's read this book over and over and has wanted to know more for all this time."

"Yeah, I can see he's been reading it. Look how dog-eared it is! He must have it memorized by now."

"Not quite, but he's read enough to have lots of questions. He's already decided this is the truth. Five years! Isn't that something? I knew nothing about it ...."

Jeff agreed. "Wow! No wonder he was so excited when he heard you preach. It's like God sort of gave him a preview five years ago to get him ready for the real thing!"

They talked on through the night. Jeff curled up on one of the big wooden beds and dozed. It was early morning when Fraser awakened him and said they were ready to leave.

"Moh has a ton of questions to ask, but I can't stay now. We have to be up the valley by midday. But I promised to come back in a few days. I've never seen a man so eager to know about the Lord Jesus."

Returning to Moh's place a couple days later was like riding with a royal coach to the coronation. Talk about welcome! The eager Chinese searcher had closed his shop for as long as James could stay, so that he could spend all his time listening to this foreigner with the answers.

The eager listener had his wife prepare more food than Jeff had seen since his last Christmas, a regular feast. When it came to bedtime, Moh spread his blankets out on the floor beside James' bed.

"Is he going to sleep there all night?" Jeff asked, amazed.

"Yes. It's supposed to be a great honor to the guest to have the host sleep beside you on the floor. So I guess I'm honored," Fraser replied, laughing.

The days spent with Moh went by quickly. Mrs. Moh and the rest of the family were friendly and entertained Jeff while James and Moh talked.

"I'm sure his faith in God is genuine," Fraser said to Jeff after three days. "But I wish he'd take down the idol shelf he's got over there on the wall."

A large brass idol sat in the main room with incense burning in front of it. Day and night the incense was kept burning. Fraser mentioned it to Moh. He couldn't be a believer in Jesus and still cling to his old idols. Besides, a Christian had God with him; he didn't need idols.

But Moh was a afraid of what would happen to him and his family if he took it down. Gently Fraser talked to him. They knelt and prayed about it. Jeff watched as they got up and approached the image. Moh's eyes were wide with fear, and perspiration stood in beads on his face. He put out a shaking hand toward the idol shelf, then stopped.

"Come on let's pray once more," Fraser suggested. Jeff could see Moh was relieved at the suggestion. So again they prayed. This time Moh got up quickly, marched over to the idol with determination, and took down all the red paper, the Chinese characters saying Heaven and Earth, the paper money given to the gods, and finally the idol itself. Leaving the shelf bare, Moh carried everything out into the yard, setting fire to what would burn and smashing the idol until it was unrecognizable.

"He says if he's done the right thing, he'll have good dreams tonight," Fraser told Jeff as flames leaped high in the air and neighbors came to investigate the commotion. "We'll see."

In the morning as they got up to leave, James said something to Moh and the two of them laughed, slapping each other's backs in joy.

"Well?" Jeff asked, "Did he? Did he have good dreams?"

"He did indeed. He certainly did!" Fraser stuffed his extra shirt into his bag. "We'll be back here,

I just know it. I'll be spending a lot of time with Moh before I'm done, I predict. He's a man I enjoy being with, and he surely has plenty of questions to ask. But for now, we need to move on."

Jeff began to realize how good the time with Moh had been as they traipsed from village to village, finding not one Lisu ready to believe. Though many were friendly, no one wanted to turn to God. People were waiting to see what happened to those who had already believed, like Mr. and Mrs. Tsai and family in Tantsah. Would God protect them from the evil spirits they had offended? If so, others would believe too.

"It will take time," Fraser said. "Plenty of time. I mustn't try to rush things." Every letter he wrote to his mother he asked the prayer group to pray for him — not just that he would be safe climbing over the treacherous peaks or healthy in spite of existing mainly on rice, but also that Lisu people, whole families of them, would believe in Christ as their Savior from sin and their protection from the evil spirits.

Was James actually becoming discouraged? It seemed he was saying things like, "It'll take time" or "I must not rush" more and more often these days as if to boost his own sagging spirits. Jeff saw him sitting, shoulders hunched, staring off to the distant peaks, as they sat by the campfire one night. The air was chilly now that the sun had gone down, and Jeff grabbed his jacket. The weight of his tape player in the inner pocket gave him an idea.

There was no one here but James, and Jeff had come to trust him to keep a secret. It would be hard to explain, certainly, but then James already accepted the fact that there were some very unexplainable things about Jeff; he didn't pry. And though he might find it unbelievable, the engineer in him would surely be intrigued — James was the kind of man who'd appreciate something like that. Why not?

Jeff pulled out the recorder and held it on his lap. "Ever see anything like this?" Jeff pressed the "Play" button and adjusted the volume. Without the headphones, the music escaped from the built-in speaker at the back. Fraser was instantly curious.

"What on earth ...? What is that? Where's the music coming from?"

Jeff laughed. "It's a cassette player and recorder. The music is on a cassette. Here. This thing." He shut off the player and extracted the tape. "This is a cassette. The music is recorded on this ribbon sort of thing, here," he poked with his little finger, "and when you put it in and turn it on, it plays. Like this." He demonstrated again. "It sounds better if you put on these." He held out earphones for James to try.

Cautious, the tall Englishman ran his fingers

over the soft black discs before putting them in his ears. Assured that this was no plot, he listened, making no comment. In a second, his face registered awe and broke into a huge smile. Then he burst out laughing as the music poured on.

"This is wonderful! Amazing! Oh, it sounds like I'm right there in the middle of the band. Only I do wish it were a symphony instead of this wretched hodgepodge of noise!" He took off the headphones and began firing questions at Jeff.

Jeff answered them as well as he could. He explained that anything could be recorded on such a cassette and that this was merely the only one he'd brought with him. "They have some with the kind of music you'd like, too. All sorts of classical ones, everything. Too bad ... too bad you can't hear them." For an instant Jeff wished he could hop back through time and bring James back a tape that he'd enjoy. What a treat it would be to him!

"Look, I'll show you what we can do." He could always record this over again when he got home, he decided. Might as well let James have some fun for now. He pushed the "Record" button. "There. Now say something. Say ... a Bible verse in Chinese or something. Anything."

Fraser looked at Jeff, hesitating for a moment, then he put his mouth down very close to the machine and began to talk. "No, not so close. It's got a built-in mike, it'll pick you up. Just say it normally."

"It has what? What are you talking about?"

"A mike — microphone. The thing that amplifies your voice. It's built right in, it'll pick up all the sounds around it, you don't need to get too close."

Fraser shook his head, baffled. Then he moved the recorder further from his mouth, cleared his throat and started again. "John 3:16: For God so loved the world ...," he recited. Jeff played it back, and James listened with amazement as his voice came back to him, saying the verse first in English, then in Chinese. "Now let me say it in Lisu," he said. Jeff pushed "Record" again and Fraser said the same verse in Lisu. "Can we sing onto it? Come on!" He cleared his throat and lifted his head. "God save our gracious king, long live our noble king," his voice rang out, louder now, echoing from the hills on all sides. He was clearly getting to like this idea! Jeff tried to sing along with him, humming the tune when he didn't know the words.

"Okay, you had yours," Jeff said, laughing. "Now it's my turn. Come on — 'O-oh say can you see, by the dawn's early light,'" he began. Together they sang through piece after piece, laughing and whooping, singing and imitating bird calls, recording and erasing and recording again.

Jeff had never seen James have so much fun. What a difference it would make to him if he could have one of these for himself. Too bad he was born half a century too early.

"I don't understand it," Fraser said finally. "I've never seen such a machine. I'm quite sure we don't have them in England. Is this some ... some American thing?"

Jeff shrugged. "I don't know. No, not really. It's just — it's kinda, kinda new. I mean, they'll have them in England too, just not yet. I can't explain it, but I thought you'd enjoy it."

"Oh, I do indeed. It's super! What a marvelous instrument! I am hoping to bring some recording equipment back with me from England next time I go, to make some radio programs for the Lisu. But I've never seen anything like this. If I do, I'll have to get one."

Jeff swallowed. "Well, you might not see one like this. This is a special kind, ... kind of expensive. I don't really want everyone to see it; that's why I've kept it hidden."

"Of course. I understand. For one thing, they wouldn't understand anyway, and for another, it might very easily get stolen. You're wise to keep it out of sight. I won't say anything about it, but thank you for showing me." Fraser sat, smiling to himself as Jeff put away his recorder.

After a while the tall missionary shook his head and said slowly, "Hmmm. Human voice ... in a compact instrument where it could be carried anywhere and played back, even without the speaker being present, if necessary. Jeff, do you realize what potential this has? For language study, for instance. One could record the words directly as the native speakers say them, then play them over and over for memorizing, or take them home to refer to when translating the Scriptures or — Or one could record songs sung in one village so that the next village could learn from them."

"Yes. I know. It has lots of uses. They use it for —" Jeff stopped. There was no sense opening up a whole mysterious world of technology that Fraser would never see. He added lamely, "For all sorts of things."

"And I could make a recording of Lisu voices and take it home to England to let my mother hear what their language sounds like." Fraser was getting more excited as he went along. They talked on into the night. Jeff was glad he had showed Fraser the instrument, but that was enough. From now on, it goes back into hiding. The more people who saw it, the more chance there was of someone finding it "useful." He didn't want anyone getting ideas.

The two were just about to drop off to sleep, when James announced. "Tomorrow we'll meet Ah-Do again. He's going to escort us for a few days through Kachin country."

"Okay," is all Jeff said. But he silently wondered if that was supposed to be some kind of warning. Who were the Kachin?

EIGHT

The People They Call Wild

"Look at this, Jeff. Isn't it marvelous?"

They were walking along the side of a steep gorge now, almost 8,000 feet above sea level. Just over the mountain ridge on the left was the land of Burma. Ah-Do had joined them again for a few days of trekking through new territory.

"The Kachin live above the rivers in that direction," Fraser explained, pointing with his chin.

"Who are the Kachin? Are they fierce or something?" Jeff wanted to know.

"People call them the 'wild Kachin,'" Fraser answered. They're not cannibals, but that's about all you can say for them. They're dirty, ignorant, warlike people. They fight with everybody else, and everybody fights with them."

"Sound like real nice folks."

"The Lisu don't like them, and vice-versa. They're robbers, for one thing. All the tribes have arrows, and the Kachin are skilled marksmen. But the Lisu put poison on their arrows, and that's the only thing that keeps the Kachin away. If they weren't afraid of those poison arrows, they would stop at nothing."

Jeff stared. This was unbelievable. Arrows? Wild Kachin? "Well, if these people are so fierce, why are we headed for their villages?"

"I've been doing sort of a census among the Lisu, recording distances between villages, the altitude, travel conditions," Fraser explained. "Helps to get a handle on the task ahead in bringing them the Gospel. Now we want to do the same among the Kachin. Not one of them, as far as we know, has ever heard of the Lord Jesus Christ."

"Oh," said Jeff.

"We'll be careful," James said, turning to hear what Ah-Do was saying in Lisu.

"Look, Jeff, a Kachin village!"

Neither Jeff nor James had seen the shacks on the hillside ahead until Ah-Do alerted Fraser. Unlike the Lisu houses, these were up on stilts. Goats, pigs and chickens lived underneath. "I will say this," Fraser said, "the Kachin have bamboo floors in their houses at least. A little better than the dirt floors the Lisu have."

Suddenly from out of nowhere, a whirling sound whizzed past Jeff's ear. The teenager turned suddenly to see an arrow stuck in the ground behind him. Fraser wasn't kidding! "Look at this," he shouted.

There wasn't time for looking. From the same hidden source another arrow came flying, barely missing James' head.

"Quick! Run for those rocks," Fraser shouted.

Ah-Do was ducking behind a large rock now, and Jeff and Fraser were right behind him. The outcropping of granite that rose from beside the path at that point was barely big enough to shelter the three beseiged travelers, but it was better than nothing. As more arrows flew their way, the tall Britisher, the squat Lisu, and the long-legged American teenager squeezed so tightly together that they could hear each others' hearts pounding.

Peering carefully around the edge of the stone blind, Fraser saw a movement in the bushes. "Over there. There's a man in the bushes over there. No, wait a minute, two, no, three, four men. There they are. I see them now. Yes, they're Kachin all right. You can tell them by their strange baggy pantaloons."

Jeff stayed hidden, squashed between Ah-Do and Fraser. A prickly bush behind kept his face and knees pressed against the rock shield.

As the three huddled out of sight, the Kachin voices faded. The sound of their footsteps told Jeff the four marksmen were heading back to their village. They had given up. Once Jeff was sure the Kachin were at a safe distance, he straightened up and peered over the rock outcropping. Raising himself on tiptoes, he stretched until he could see the backs of the four attackers. Sure enough, their strange white cloth pants were made in such a way that the seat of them drooped down to mid-calf. The legs were short, just below the knees.

Fraser climbed out onto the pathway. "That was a close one. Those men probably just wanted to keep us away from their village, not kill us — not today, anyway. I told you they were wild folks."

"Wild is right! Some people you've got up here!" *Brother!* Jeff thought, *it's like being in a cowboy movie, hiding behind rocks while someone shoots arrows at you!*

"I think we'd better steer clear of that village. There were about twenty houses."

There was no sign of the Kachin attackers as the three foreign intruders followed the trail around a bulge in the mountainside. The forest was thicker here and the rocks more rugged. The fog had enclosed them again. They climbed over a rocky ridge and jumped across a stream that had overflowed its narrow banks.

Suddenly James slowed and motioned for Jeff and Ah-Do to stay behind him. Now what? In a small cave by the side of the road just ahead

Jeff could see three grubby men with matted hair bent over their work. As one of them lifted his head and spat out some red liquid, Jeff could see that each cradled a crude weapon on his lap. "That one near the fire, there," Fraser pointed out, whispering, "he's fixing opium to smoke. The one on this side looks like he's got a gun of some kind. Better be careful."

Jeff was just going to say, "Yea, and the other guys have knives or something," when Fraser stepped into the open and waved a hand in greeting.

Suddenly the leader jumped up from his work and confronted Fraser. His sharp black eyes narrowed with hatred. Waving a small sword in the air, the man scowled and spat out a string of words. A scar on his forehead just over his left eye gave the impression that this wasn't going to be his first fight. One of his companions jumped from rock to rock, landing just in front of Jeff with a chilling yell.

Jeff froze. Where could he run? There was nowhere to hide. Besides, this guy and his hench-men/buddies could easily overpower all three of them if they moved a muscle. Jeff stood welded to the spot.

Jabbering something, the Kachin suddenly each grabbed an intruder. Fraser's attacker was the one with the sword. The one holding Ah-Do had a dagger, Jeff's captor the old-fashioned rifle. While such an ancient piece of armament as that gun would have aroused Jeff's curiosity under normal conditions, at this point he was conscious only of the rusty barrel focused right on his chest.

The leader of the trio was waving his sword at James and holding out one hand. *Maybe he's saying "give me all your money or I'll dice you into coleslaw,"* Jeff thought.

"I don't know what they're saying," Fraser said calmly to Jeff. "I don't speak Kachin. But I understand the word 'money.' I think they want to rob us. It wouldn't be the first time."

Jeff found anger replacing his fear. *They want to rob us! Great! So they do this regularly, do they? That makes it all right? Come on. Let's get out of here!* While he was thinking this, the talking continued. The Kachin exchanged loud, excited words among themselves, occasionally directing demands, apparently, at Fraser. Not even Ah-Do understood Kachin; so he couldn't intervene.

Then as Jeff watched, Ah-Do began to undo his Chinese jacket. "We have nothing to give them," Fraser was saying calmly. "I have only a few coins for use in the towns we enter, not enough to satisfy them. Ah-Do thinks we may be able to buy them off by offering our clothes. It's all, I think, we can do." As he began to strip off his shirt too, Jeff watched in amazement.

What are we going to do? Stand here in our underwear? Jeff thought. *Not me. I'm going to make these guys see that we aren't worth robbing!*

He fumbled in his pockets for something he could part with. "Look, how about it if I give you —" His right pocket was empty. He pulled it inside out to prove it. The leader took a step closer till the gun poked Jeff's stomach.

Jeff was glad he'd put his cassette player inside his jacket and shirt, around his neck, next to his skin, where it was well hidden from view. He wouldn't want to have to give these gangsters that. The gunbarrel kept poking menacingly.

"Okay, Okay! Just a minute!" *I must have some stuff on me, I hope, I hope. Oooh, come on, be there — something, anything!* Jeff thought frantically. His pants pocket yielded one quarter. He tried to smile as he handed it over. "There. See? One quarter. Twenty-five cents. You can have it. I don't need it anyhow."

Jeff continued to fumble frantically. "Here, you can have this too." He pulled out a pack of bubble gum. "Go ahead." He dropped it in the dirty palm of the leader with the glinty eyes. The man looked at it, curious. His face softened slightly as he fingered the amazing object. He ran his fingers over the smooth, thick packaging, mystified. Jeff helped his attacker open the package and slide out a piece of gum. He pointed to his mouth to indicate chewing.

The man watched, nodded, then quickly remembered his business and turned his attention back to Jeff. The gun, which had lowered just an inch or two was now jerked into position again at Jeff's stomach muscles. The shrill-voiced man repeated something he'd said before.

Jeff felt for more tradeable treasures. "Here, look what I found. You can have it." He wiggled a paper from his jacket pocket. It was a Sunday-school paper, folded in quarters and stuffed into his pocket one Sunday in his rush to get out the door after class. He hadn't even glanced at it enough to know what the story was.

"Here — a paper. See you can open it, like this. And it has pictures." He pointed out its appeal and put it in the man's dirty hand along with the gum.

"That's all. I haven't got anything else to give you. Honest. That's it." He spread out his hands and hoped the man believed him. His fingers were icy, and he had to lock his knees to stop them from shaking. During all this Fraser and Ah-Do had stood motionless, held to the spot by the weapons trained on them. Besides, as Fraser said later, Jeff seemed to be making his point; no sense in jumping in and spoiling everything. Jeff glanced at Fraser, whose eyes told him to stand still and see what would happen.

Then the fiercest-looking of the three bandits

grabbed Jeff's shoulder and shook him, putting his dirty face close to Jeff's and yelling something at him. The man apparently hadn't bathed for years, and his breath was as foul as his body. Jeff got a grim look at broken black teeth as the man leaned close to make his point. He was pointing down the road now toward the village ahead.

Just then a man came running down the hill toward them. He shouted something as he approached, and the three villains backed away, lowering their weapons and muttering angrily.

The newcomer smiled broadly and began a rapid explanation to James in Chinese. James smiled in return and winked at Jeff.

"He says he came to the mission home in Tengyueh once and met me there," James explained as they walked, "though I don't remember his face. Anyway, he's not afraid of us and apologizes for the unfriendly welcome. He says we're to spend the night with him."

Fraser and Ah-Do exchanged a few short sentences in Lisu, quickly agreeing to the man's offer. Jeff wasn't quite sure it was a safe thing to do, but he had no choice. Once in the village, however, Jeff gradually lost his suspicion. The Kachin proved to be friendly and hospitable. They listened eagerly to Fraser, and the next morning they escorted the three travelers to the edge of the village, smiling and bowing politely.

"D'you know we counted three hundred villages and at least ten thousand Lisu on this trip, and even more Kachin," Fraser said one morning as they waited for the coffee to heat over Ah-Do's open fire. "And we haven't even started to count other tribes like the Shan — and the Wa. And that's only in this direction. If we were to travel further, I'm sure we'd find thousands more."

"Yeah, there's lots of them, all right. Nobody's ever counted them? I mean doesn't the government know how many there are?"

"Almost impossible to count. We are very likely the first Westerners ever to visit here. And certainly there are no Christians among them except the few we know. Imagine — thousands, and no one bothering to spread the Gospel among them. I can't get over that. I can't visit every village — even every *Lisu* village. If people would only obey God's call to leave home and jobs to reach these people! If only we could teach the Lisu to read and had the Scriptures in Lisu to leave with them. The Word of God can work without us."

Jeff nodded. "Like with Moh."

"Exactly. Getting the Bible into Lisu may be the most important thing I can ever do."

Jeff nodded. He was surprised to find that he was beginning to share Fraser's enthusiasm. What was important to Fraser was becoming important to him. But he was tired. Not just tired of walking. Tired of traipsing over mountains, of rabid dogs, quicksand, flying arrows, and robbers. He was glad that God hadn't called him to this kind of life!

NINE
The Paper Talks Lisu

"We're coming close to Six Family Hollow," Fraser said, pointing to a tiny patch of thatch on the hill ahead. "Ah-Do's home. Remember? His mother, Mrs. Tsai, was the Lisu lady who stuck up for you when you tangled with Liang Tingwu."

How could he forget! But, fascinated with the name of the village, Jeff asked, "What a name! Do only six families live there?"

"Only three, actually. Mr. and Mrs. Tsai and family plus two more."

Their Lisu companion began quickening his steps as they neared Six Family Hollow. "Ah-Do will leave us here," Fraser explained. Jeff liked Ah-Do. He just wished he could talk to him.

"We'll have to stop and see the family, at least

have a meal, and maybe spend the night. Mrs. Tsai will insist."

Jeff thought he noticed a discouraged tone under Fraser's seemingly optimistic words. *Was the excitement of mountain travel beginning to wear off for him too?* Jeff wondered. *Maybe it's the disappointment of being so close to Tantsah and yet not being allowed to go there.*

Mrs. Tsai came out to meet them before they got into the village clearing. She greeted Fraser warmly.

As they walked toward the shack this Christian family called home, with pigs and chickens scuttling out of the way with every step, Ah-Do and his mother talked excitedly. Seems there was some news since they'd been on the road.

James turned to Jeff when there was a break in the conversation. "Well, good news. It seems it's safe for us to return to Tantsah now. They say the Chinese authorities have said we can go and live there and teach." Fraser's thin face was lit with a big smile for the first time in days.

Jeff was happy for Fraser, but skeptical. "What about ol' Crab-Face — I mean Liang Tingwu? You think he changed his mind?"

"No. I doubt if Liang Tingwu likes us any better than before, but he's willing to let us come. Mrs. Tsai says the headman, who has some in-fluence with Liang, has offered to let us live in his house."

Fraser was eager to get going when he heard the news. But Mrs. Tsai wouldn't let them leave without a meal. When she had the room smoky enough to call out the fire department if there'd been one, she called everyone to supper. Jeff sat down beside the youngest son in the family and let Mrs. Tsai heap generous portions of rice and cabbage on to a tin plate for him. She seemed to think he needed fattening up. Then she reached into a pot and pulled out a small piece of chicken with chopsticks. Smiling proudly, she placed it on top of Jeff's rice, the finishing touch to a perfect meal.

When supper was finished, Jeff sat in the shadows and watched Fraser, squatting next to the fire, reading from his Chinese Bible and explaining it to the family. No matter how eager Fraser was to move on to Tantsah, he'd never pass up a chance like this. He answered questions and taught the family to respond with answers to catechism-like questions. "Is it wrong to worship the demons?" he would ask, for example.

"It is very wrong," everyone would respond in chorus.

One by one neighbors gathered. The house filled quickly, and a spill-over crowd stood outside the door. Jeff didn't know what James was saying, but he saw by the way he was pointing to his Chinese Bible and stumbling for words that he must be reading them the Bible in Chinese and translating it into Lisu. No one seemed perturbed by the smoke, and no one seemed to tire of listening. On and on Fraser talked. Sometimes someone would ask a question, and Fraser would answer.

Then Mrs. Tsai began the notes of a song. In a moment everyone was singing. They had sung only a few bars when Jeff recognized the song — "Jesus Loves Me." Where on earth did they learn "Jesus Loves Me"? It was not very harmonious, but within minutes, James had corrected the wrong notes and worked on the timing. *That's the professional musician in him,* Jeff thought — *James couldn't be satisfied with less than a perfect sound.*

Now Fraser introduced a song he had written in Lisu. He'd taught it to other villages too — something about God being stronger than the spirits. They sang it over and over. Jeff hummed along. Before he knew it, they were not only singing the tune, but adding harmony parts as well. Ah-Do now took up a tenor, the son over there on the far side must be singing bass — yes, one by one, they added parts till the whole song ended in great harmony. *Like a choir,* Jeff thought. *Fraser was right — the Lisu could sing!*

Then it was Mrs. Tsai's turn to talk. James smiled as he listened. More singing, more questions, more answers. Jeff was drifting off to sleep by the time Fraser shook him and led him to the lean-to outside that had been designated as guest room.

"I must tell you what Mrs. Tsai told me tonight," James said as Jeff snuggled into his blanket for the night.

"You saw the big old pig snorting around by the door when we came in?" Jeff nodded. "Well, that pig is her pride and joy — as it is for any Lisu that owns such a grand possession. And it's valuable too — worth a lot of money to these people. Well, it seems that pig has wandered off three times. Each time Mrs. Tsai prayed, and each time the pig came home! Now she's convinced that prayer works. In fact, she wants to show us in the morning how even her pig prays!" James chuckled. "I don't know about that, but we'll see."

The sun had barely risen over the mountain when Jeff and James folded their blankets and packed to leave. "We'll be in Tantsah in a short while. But first we mustn't disappoint Mrs. Tsai. Let's go see her praying pig!"

Chuckling, Mrs. Tsai grabbed Jeff's arm and led them outside the door. She threw a bucket of slop in the pig's trough, and as they watched, amused, the pig laid his head oddly to one side and leaned it on the trough, eyes closed. Then in a minute it opened its eyes and began to eat.

Mrs. Tsai was laughing and jabbering all at once. "See," Fraser interpreted, "even my pig prays!'" And all three of them laughed.

"Weirdest thing," chuckled Jeff, running his fingers through his hair, sticky with soot. "I've never seen a pig do that!"

"She just wants to prove all her household have been truly following the Lord," Fraser said as they left the village, headed for Tantsah. "Her faith has held that family together over a lot of problems these past months. They've had sickness, opposition, all sorts of things, but she's never wavered. She's a grand, saintly lady."

As they neared Tantsah, James seemed almost to break into a run. "At last we are going to live in Tantsah. This is the place to be, I know it is. Living here will prove to be the answer. Now we'll begin to see all the Lisu in the area turn to Christ, I'm sure."

Jeff hoped he was right. He could see how hopeful Fraser was. He felt some of Fraser's excitement rubbing off on him as they neared the town. Things were going to get better now!

"Let's go see the room the headman has for us."

Jeff realized with dismay that the room was a loft over the main floor of the house. It was too low for Fraser to stand upright, stiflingly hot, and unbelievably dirty. Rats scurried away as they entered. Besides that, the floor boards were loose and spaced so far apart you'd lose anything you dropped through the crack.

"What a dive!" he complained in a whisper to James. "We can't live here. Are you really going to stay in a place like this?"

"I have nowhere else. As long as I'm living here with the Lisu I came to teach, I don't care what kind of house it is."

"Oh, brother!" Jeff muttered.

"Besides," James added, "we can hear all the conversation down below, and that will be good language practice. Think how much more quickly I'll learn to speak Lisu! You might even learn some yourself."

Jeff snorted. "You bet we'll hear their conversation. And they'll hear ours. And a lot of other things. I'm not staying in a pigsty." He swatted angrily at a spider that descended in front of him.

"Maybe you'd better eat before you make such a decision. It's time for supper. Come along."

Jeff threw his jacket on their pile of stuff in the corner, making sure it didn't drag on the filthy floor and stomped down the ladder after Fraser. What a place!

The family seemed friendly. They certainly talked freely. Jeff found it hard to stay disgrunted when he could see that James was delighted to be there. And with a sigh, he plunked down beside the rumpled pioneer on a log beside the fire. The hostess bent over a pot, stirring something steamy, jewelry jangling with each move of her body. Her long earrings almost touched the rising steam. Jeff accepted the plate of rice she handed him.

Then when she had given Fraser a similar amount, she reached into another pot and carefully picked out a piece of meat and placed it on top of Fraser's rice. She smiled and chatted as she did the same for Jeff. Jeff could tell from the expressions of the children around him they considered him lucky to have such a delicacy. The misplaced teenager couldn't quite identify the piece — it didn't quite look like chicken, and it wasn't pork.

"What is it?" he whispered to Fraser when the conversation occupied his hosts. "Is it okay to eat?"

Fraser looked at him and winked a long slow wink. His mouth twitched at the corners, but that was the only hint of a smile as he said, "It's perfectly okay. It's rat. Nicely stewed."

"No! Are you serious? It's not, is it?"

"Sssh. Don't make a scene. Yes, it is. I've had it often in Lisuland." Fraser smiled and winked again, taking a slow, grateful bite of the creature on top of his rice. "Just don't think about it and mix it in well — you'll never notice."

"Oh, no!" Jeff tried to keep from bolting as he slipped off the log and out the door. He rushed to the shadows behind the house and fought with his boiling stomach. He couldn't hold it down any longer. He leaned over a stump on the edge of the clearing and was immediately, thoroughly sick. The darkness covered and calmed him somewhat as he wiped off his face and leaned against a tree trunk, willing himself to stop shaking. He knew they were laughing at him inside the house. Well, let them! He wasn't about to eat rat!

Jeff lay awake on the bumpy floorboards a long time that night. Though his stomach had settled down, his mind was racing. He hated it here. He wasn't exactly used to luxury — after all his family just lived a normal middle-class life. And he was always happy for adventure or trying something new. But this — this was too much! In the first place if it weren't for Zeke's stupid mistake, he wouldn't even be here. And then as if that weren't enough, he had left what might have been a decent home in Tengyueh to live in this dirty hovel with no one who spoke English or understood him — except J. O. Fraser, and he seemed to care more about his precious Lisu than about Jeff.

Jeff longed for a plate of decent American food. Oh for some Geovanni's pizza! Or Wheat Thins and pimento cheese! Even a vegetable quiche with mushrooms would be better than this! Rat! Ugh!

And to make matters worse, there was nothing he could do about his predicament. He'd learned from his previous experience that he couldn't bring himself back. It depended on Zeke reversing the process with his machine-thing back in Illinois. All he could do was make life as pleasant as possible where he was in the meantime. And maybe, if possible, to be of some use.

Well, being of use was out of the question. He was more of a nuisance than anything. Of course, that's what he'd thought last time too .... Even if Zeke didn't know what he was doing, and nobody else had any idea how to help him, God did.

Hey, why hadn't he thought of that sooner? God wasn't affected by where he was or what year it was. God was the same all the time. Right? So maybe God could help him even in a weird situation like this.

He raised up on one elbow and looked over at James, who snored peacefully on the floor beside him. *Nothing bothers that man! He actually likes living up here,* he thought ruefully. Shaking his head, he flopped back down on his thin blanket and pulled a corner of it over his shoulders.

Of course, James was being nice to him and trying to help him. He realized that. Couldn't blame James. And really, if he was honest, he had to admit his host and hostess were being kind to him too. The lady had no idea he wouldn't like rat! She thought she was doing him a favor. A grim grin came to his face. Funny kind of favor!

To Jeff's relief, even Fraser was happy a few days later when the Lisu arranged for him to have a house of his own.

"How's that for a palace?" Fraser said to Jeff, as they moved into the structure that had been provided for them. "Two rooms, a view, my books, and a good companion. What more could a man ask for?"

Jeff grinned. "I could think of a few things. What about a bathroom for starters? With hot water."

"Oh, we can bathe in that river down there."

"That river's racing! Besides, then you have to climb 2000 feet back up afterward. Not a good solution. And how about furniture? Or food?"

"Furniture we can make out of trees, or do without. As for food, I did bring some cocoa this time, and some condensed milk. I always get so hungry for something sweet when I eat only Lisu food, so I brought the condensed milk." Jeff twisted his face. He wasn't crazy about the thick, sweet milk. Still, he had to admit, it was better than nothing. "And a tin of pears and a package of biscuits." Jeff knew by this time that "biscuits" were plain cookies in American.

"I even bought us two enameled plates and two mugs, a set for you and a set for me," Fraser said, drawing them from the box and putting them up against the wall. He coughed, and Jeff thought he saw him wince slightly as he did so. "There, now, with my books over here, we're unpacked. Just like that."

Fraser coughed again and wiped the perspiration from his face with a well-worn handkerchief though it wasn't a hot day. Fraser saw Jeff looking at him with concern. He smiled quickly. "Just a bit weak from the move, I guess. Merely temporary. I'm better already." He straightened his shoulders and gave his trousers a hike up over his thin hips.

"Better enough to be ready for visitors, I hope, 'cause it looks like we're going to have some," Jeff said peering out the door. A crowd of children approached, laughing, bracelets jingling, bobbing up and down in excitement. Obviously they hadn't seen anything as interesting as the foreigners in their lives!

Great! Jeff thought. *I suppose they're going to hang around here all day. And knowing James, he'll let them.*

He did. In fact, James Fraser seemed delighted that they'd come. After the children left, the missionary sat on the tiny porch, legs hanging over the edge, watching the sun fall behind the mountain beside him. Jeff's attempts to talk met only with silence or a non-committal grunt. Fraser wasn't much for small talk, Jeff had learned. He gave up and went to the river below for water to use for cooking supper.

Every day visitors came. Children especially.

They loved to watch the white man and boy reading and writing. *I can see the headlines now,* Jeff thought, *if they had a paper: "White man and boy make marks on paper; paper talks Lisu."* Though Fraser could speak Lisu enough to be understood, every day he tried to learn more. Constantly he was listening and writing, trying to spell words and phrases the way they would be spelled in English if they were written.

"What d'you do if they say a sound that we don't have in English?" Jeff asked.

"I make up a symbol for it by turning an English letter upside down, or backwards." Fraser wrote a backwards capital D on the paper and pronounced it to illustrate. "And because the 'ah' sound is so common, I write only the consonants for syllables using the 'ah' sound. See, like this. L is always pronounced 'la.' If there's no vowel written with it, the vowel sound is automatically 'ah.' The vowel comes at the end of every syllable — never in the middle or beginning, so everyone knows to put an 'ah' sound at the end." Other vowels he wrote in with a letter. Before long Jeff found he could read the Lisu words, even though he didn't know what they meant. He read a page and Fraser nodded approvingly.

"Exactly! See what I mean? With my system, it's easy to learn to read Lisu. You can help teach reading to some of the children too — just help them pronounce the sounds; you don't have to understand it."

"He's writing down all our language," one old man complained, misunderstanding the mysterious marks. "He's going to write it all down and take it away, and then we won't have any language to speak."

The children, however, had no such fear. They came all day, every day, and talked, listened, and laughed at the two funny creatures. One day James Fraser saw the little girl they called Fourth Sister playing with the piece of soap he had just used.

"Here's my chance," he said to Jeff, going over to the child. "Might as well show her how it's done." He poured a little water in the basin and wet the girl's hands. Then he rubbed her hand on the soap and showed her how to lather it by rubbing them together. Then he rinsed the hands, leaving them whiter than they'd been since she was born. The girl looked in delight. Her eyes registered her amazement.

"You're a magician," Jeff said. "She looked at you like you'd just pulled a rabbit out of a hat or turned a one dollar bill into a ten."

In no time, the others wanted the same experience. So Jeff got busy too, wetting, rubbing, lathering, rinsing, drying, until each one in turn had hands a dozen times cleaner than their bodies.

"You know that's probably the first time

they've ever seen soap — they use ashes instead, if they use anything," Fraser told him. "They never bathe, you know."

"I can see why, when you have to go down to the river hundreds of feet below to do it." Jeff had seen Fourth Sister's mother doing the laundry. It meant carrying the dirty clothes down to the river far below, sousing them up and down in the water, then spreading each piece out on the ground and walking on it with bare feet to loosen the dirt. Then she'd rinsed it again and spread it on a rock to dry. "It's a lot of work to keep clean when you have to do it their way."

Writing fascinated the children most. As James put a book on the floor in front of him one day, the kids immediately crowded around, running their fingers over the paper and letters, pronouncing the words they recognized, waiting for a prompt when they didn't. "That little girl, Fourth Sister, is so smart," Fraser said to Jeff, "that she has the idea already."

"So do some of the others," responded Jeff. He really enjoyed the expressions of wonder and satisfaction that crossed their faces when the Lisu kids were able to read what was written. And, just as Fraser had said, Jeff found he could help them even without knowing a lot of Lisu himself.

"The Chinese insist you can't teach a Lisu to read," James said. "They say it's impossible to teach the 'monkey people' anything. Obviously the Chinese are wrong. I think that with my simple script even most adults could learn in no time. Look how eager the children are!"

Fraser measured water from the bucket into a pot to cook the rice for supper. "That ought to be enough for you. I'm not hungry. I'll just have a cup of tea." Jeff wanted to object but knew it would do no good.

Fraser had other things on his mind. He sat on his sleeping mat in the corner and began to write, as he so often did. "Another letter to your mom?" Jeff asked, aware that Fraser would say "mum," not "mom" — Jeff just couldn't do it.

"Yes, but not just for Mother, this time. This is to the nine friends who pray for me in her home every month. My prayer partners, I call them. I've been thinking a lot about prayer — different kinds of prayer — and I want to tell them. It occurred to me that definite prayer — what I call the prayer of faith — is similar to an English man moving to the West, say to Canada, for instance, to claim land and build a farm there. There are lots of similarities. For instance, there's lots of room for him in Canada, and the government encourages settlers. They offer cheap fares and free land — they want people to come and claim it. And yet there are limits too. He can't just go anywhere he wants and stake his claim to thousands of miles. D'you see what I mean? In praying there's plenty to ask for, plenty to expect God to do by faith, and God tells us to ask. But there are limits. God isn't going to give us any old thing we claim.

"Around here, for example, in Tantsah district alone, there are more than two thousand families of Lisu, aren't there? Well, I've been praying that several hundred families will become Christians. That's not too much to ask, it seems to me.

"I'm going to tell my prayer partners this, ask them to pray for the same thing."

He wrote quickly now. "October 9, 1915 — My dear friends ...."

Jeff nodded. He hadn't thought of prayer like that before. But it made sense. God did want his children to ask. And Fraser's request was surely not unreasonable. Seems like God would certainly answer. Maybe now, with everyone praying, things would start to change. Jeff was feeling a little bit excited. In fact, he hardly knew what to expect.

TEN

Caught

Sunshine filtered through the pine trees around the bamboo-and-grass cabin. A bird repeated its song from the nearest branch as Fraser called Jeff to breakfast. The fourteen-year old pulled on his loose Chinese trousers that Fraser had found for him, grabbed a bucket, and ran down the hill to the creek bubbling below. He splashed water over his face and scooped up a load to carry back to the house. He was used to the rugged routine by now. Actually it made him feel good to think he could survive here just about as well as James could.

James'll love today, Jeff thought. *I bet he'll be singing when I get back to the house. He won't be able to feel depressed very long on a day like this.*

"Great day!" Jeff said as he set the bucket of water down by the little fire that served as a stove. "I beat you to the 'shower' today — I can't believe it."

But James only nodded and smiled. He'd been strangely quiet for days. His hearty, energetic laugh had stopped. Jeff found himself struggling to lighten the cloud that seemed to sit over the tiny house. He didn't know how to bring up the subject.

But today when the usual children had come and gone and the village had settled for a quiet afternoon, James sat by himself on the porch, Bible open on his lap, staring off to the mountains. Jeff dangled his feet over the side of the porch and tried for the third time to cut a whistle out of wood. If he could finish it by tomorrow, he'd give it to Fourth Sister as a reward for her reading.

"You'd think there'd be more results," Fraser said suddenly.

"I know," Jeff agreed.

"I've trekked up and down this area for months — years, in fact — preached in villages and by firesides, given out more literature than I can imagine, talked, taught, answered questions, lived like the Lisu in every way possible. The Lisu even say they're interested in hearing the Gospel. Yet very few of these people have believed. You'd think after all the effort, there'd be more to show for it."

Jeff put down the stick in his hand. So Fraser was feeling it too. He'd wondered himself how long a person could keep living like this without getting discouraged. "But some have become Christians. What about the Tsais, for example? And the Moh family — of course, they are Chinese. But other Lisu, here and there, have believed — you've told me so."

"Oh, yes, there are a few. But of the thousands of Lisu scattered all over these mountains, there should be many more. I want to see, not one or two, but hundreds, families, villages, all be- coming Christian. And that includes getting rid of their demon worship too. When I was in Burma for those weeks working with Ba Thaw, I spent a lot of time praying, really asking God for many families to become Christians. I felt that's what God wanted. And I asked my prayer partners in England to pray for that too. But now ... I don't know, maybe I'm rushing things."

"Rushing things? You just said yourself you've been at it for years. That's not rushing."

"I know, but it's just that — well, maybe God isn't ready to work in this place right now. Maybe I'm pushing too hard for something that's not to be yet.

"The directors still feel I should join the esta- blished work in the eastern part of the province — in the cities on the lower plains. I thought I could justify saying 'no' by the promise of big things to happen here among the Lisu. But I was wrong. Nothing's happening. They're not going to let me stay up here doing nothing forever. If there're no results soon — Maybe I should write and tell Mr. Hoste, our director, that I'll go to Eastern Yunnan for a while — help where I'm badly needed. Maybe I'm just holding on to a personal dream."

Fraser sighed and uncurled his long legs and paced the length of the porch and back. Jeff could see it wasn't a plan he was excited about. His real interest was the Lisu — there was no doubt about that.

"You can't give up now. You've ... you've ... well, you've done so much. I mean look at how long and hard you've worked. You thought it was what God wanted you to do. And you were right — everybody knows you're made for the Lisu work."

"Not everybody."

"Well, that's what Mrs. Embery told me. She said it wouldn't be right to try to make you work somewhere else because you belong up here in the mountains with the Lisu."

Fraser smiled. "Mrs. Embery is a wonderful lady. The Emberys understand me and what I'm trying to do. But besides those two, who is there? I'll tell you who — a few women praying for me back in England. My mother's prayer group. That's all."

"But the Lisu like you. Maybe they just don't understand the truth yet."

"They understand enough to know what it means to trust in the living God instead of demons. No, I'll tell you the trouble. Fear. The Lisu are afraid. Afraid of the spirits, afraid of the Chinese, afraid of me. It's like — well like that fog, that mist that's always hanging over everything. The way it covers everything, blocks out the sunlight. Fear holds these people in a deep, clinging fog. Only the Holy Spirit can penetrate it. I feel it as plainly as I feel the mist on that mountain over there when I'm walking through it."

"So what can we do?"

There was a long silence; then James said quietly, "Wait for God to work."

That didn't sound like James O. Fraser. Usually he had plans, actions, some way out of the solution. Now he was just going to wait?

"How long? You've been waiting a long time."

"Yes. And I've been praying; so have my prayer partners at home. We'll keep on praying. I'm convinced God will answer — sometime. But maybe not for several years yet."

Fraser stood up and paced the length of the little porch a few times before he spoke again. "But how long can I go on? I'm tired of this, tired of living like a Lisu, living with nothing, slogging through mud and rapids and avalanches, fighting their rabid dogs and poison arrows, for nothing. I wouldn't mind if they'd be interested in the Gospel when they hear it, but to do all that for nothing —"

Jeff didn't know what to say. He'd never heard Fraser complain about anything. It always seemed like he enjoyed living the way he did. Now there seemed to be an anger, a frustration that Jeff hadn't seen in him before.

Not that Jeff could blame Fraser. He felt the same way himself. It was fun to camp out for a few days, but living like James did, day in, day out, was too much. Especially when you get near a village and they send the dogs to attack you, or shoot at you. But now was not the time to say it. He wanted to do something to lift James' spirits, to help him be his old buoyant self again.

"Maybe you're just tired. You had that fever last week — remember? And you haven't been eating much. You've left most of the rice at each meal for me and barely touched your cabbage these days." Even the tins of specialty items James had stashed away in the trunk for special occasions — canned cheese, jam, evaporated milk, applesauce, pears — couldn't tempt his appetite. And his clothes, never well-fitted anyway, now hung on him.

"Maybe you need to go down to Tengyueh and visit the Emberys a while. I'll stay here by myself if you want to go." He hesitated. Did he dare make this offer? Why not? It would be kind of fun to try it on his own. "I can carry on teaching the kids to read — at least for a few days."

James smiled. "Thank you. That's good of you. You're right. I am tired. And I can't seem to get any food down. I need some good home cooking. I've had all the rice I can eat for a while." He sighed and lapsed into silence again.

"I won't be gone long," he said after a few minutes. "Just a brief rest. Are you sure you'll be all right?" Fraser looked at him with concern. "Of course, Lisu friends in town will certainly be more than kind. If you need anything, they'll be quick to help. And in this weather, living is fairly easy."

"Sure. I'll do fine. You'd be surprised how good I am at living in this kind of place by now. I've learned a lot by watching you. Anyway, it's only for a short while." Jeff put more enthusiasm into his voice than he felt.

"Jeff, just one thing," Fraser said as he was preparing to leave town, "you know that little record-player box you have, that ... what d'you call it?"

"Walkman cassette player and recorder."

"Yes, that. Well, if I were you, I'd try to keep it out of sight. I know you've been doing that all along, but just be extra careful with me gone. You don't want it to be stolen." Fraser hesitated, then decided to say what was on his mind. "If the Chinese authorities were to see it, who knows what they might think? A way of communicating with Britain, or — who knows? They're fearful of us anyway, suspicious. I may be overly cautious, but, just in case."

"Don't worry. I have no intention of letting anyone see it."

Fraser waved goodbye as he began the long trek toward Tengyueh. Well, a bit of Mrs. Embery's cooking would do him good. And a chance to play the organ again wouldn't hurt either.

The next few days Jeff carried on the routine they had established. Fraser had assured him he was welcome to open the tins of special food items if he wanted them; so he boiled rice and eggs and greens as usual and then added soft, orange cheese. Sometimes Koh-ma or one of the other women brought him cooked chicken or pig to add to his meal. It was kind of fun planning your own day and cooking your own food.

Housekeeping was easy, sweep the dirt out the door and roll up your sleeping bag in the morning. If he wanted to wash his shirt, he simply scrubbed it with a bit of soap in the stream down the hill and spread it on a rock for the sun to dry. Wow, if only his mom could see him now! She'd never believe it. He was surprised himself at how much he had adjusted to living there.

Fourth sister came every day as usual, followed by a gang of giggling, chattering, filthy children.

Jeff wasn't sure he should let them into the house without James there to keep an eye on things. So he pulled the books out to the porch and began the reading lesson there, with Fourth Sister sitting on her heels, her feet flat on the bamboo slats of the porch and himself sitting with legs dangling over the edge.

Not only Fourth Sister, but several of the accompanying throng were learning quickly. They could almost read and understand a whole sentence at a time. Jeff enjoyed watching their faces as the talking paper made sense to them. Too bad there wasn't something more for them to read besides just a few basic questions and answers that Fraser called a catechism and a few chapters of Mark's Gospel. Well, Fraser would soon work on that when he went to Burma next summer.

But in spite of enjoying the carefree living and the smiles of the kids, Jeff found himself more and more frustrated. What use was all their effort when, for the most part, the Lisu carried on unchanged? It was a waste of time and energy. Look what it was doing to Fraser. He was healthy and athletic when he first came here. Now he could hardly drag himself around. And all for what? Almost none of the Lisu wanted to give up their worship of spirits and call themselves Christians. Well, Fraser was finally ready to change his mind and work in the East. It was about time!

If Fraser did go to the city, living conditions

would be better. Like in Tengyueh. Jeff could live there with him. If he didn't, well, Jeff would have to go on his own. Enough of this.

Jeff had a lot of time to think in the long, lightless evenings. He'd stay, he decided, till Fraser came back and see that he was all right, of course. Then he'd try again to find a way home. He couldn't wait forever for Zeke. There must be something he could do to speed up the process. Or at least have a decent place to live in the meantime. Yes, as soon as James Fraser got back and didn't need him, he'd leave.

Also in the evenings, when the villagers were in their own houses and Jeff was sure of being alone, he would pull his tape player out of its hiding place, lay on the bed, earphones in his ears and listen to his cassette. Too bad he hadn't brought another tape with him. Maybe his new one of Buddy Storm or The Princes. He listened for the umpteenth time to "Change Up." He knew just when the music would stop and Fraser's voice would come on, reading John 3:16 in Chinese, then in Lisu. Then there was a click, a few seconds of music again, then Jeff's own voice saying, "Okay, it's recording. Now try it." He grinned. There was a big whooping noise at this point where Fraser had tried out some odd sounds. A duck call, a whistle, then Jeff's voice saying, "Hey, I know what ..." and then Fraser singing a Lisu hymn and Jeff singing it in English. Then music resumed. He could recite it all by heart.

Jeff marked off another day on the calendar. Fraser had been gone a week now. He was probably feeling a lot better already. It was hot today. Lisu who weren't working in their fields seemed to be sprawling in the shade. No one was moving about. Jeff was glad of the chance to curl up on the sleeping mat he used for a bed and have a little time to himself. He leafed through one of the magazines Fraser had in his trunk. The date on it was June 1911. He'd seen it half a dozen times already. Besides it was only black and white and all about the coronation of King George V in England. He tossed it aside. Fraser had better come back soon.

It was a relief to hear the familiar, heavy footstep on the porch a few days later. Now maybe they could pack up and clear out of here.

When the welcoming party had scattered to their homes that evening, James told Jeff about his trip, his visit with the Emberys, who fed him and listened to him and let him play the organ for hours. "I feel so much better, Jeffrey. That was what I needed. Sometimes we just overtax the old body, and it rebels, I guess. I've even gained weight already, look at these pants."

But best of all, James went on, was his visit to his friend Moh Tingchang. "That man is a wonderful believer, Jeff. It was so refreshing to visit him for a few days. I wrote a letter to Mother while I was there," he chuckled now at the thought, "and he watched me the whole time. He kept asking me, 'Is your mother a Christian too? Can she read like Mrs. Embery? What is her venerable age?' and on and on. He couldn't get over a mother as old as mine who can read and who is also a Christian!"

"Isn't his mother a believer?"

"No way! as you say. She's an opium addict. She has never forgiven him for leaving the way of the spirits and turning to Christ. She feels he's disgraced the family for generations. Tried to drown herself a while ago. She didn't go through with it — she's still alive — but she's a real trial to Moh."

James unpacked more tins of specialty goods he had brought back. "To replenish what I'm sure you ate," he laughed. "And here's some sugar." Jeff was glad to see that. They hadn't had sugar since leaving Tengyueh. The Lisu honey was a fair substitute, but it was dark and strong, not like the Sue Bee they had at home.

"But now I'll tell you what I've been thinking. I made a decision while I was at Moh's. Since there's so much work to be done everywhere else, I can't stay on here just hoping for something to happen that isn't going to. I'm going to make one more trip around Lisuland. One more. Then if there's still no response, I'm going to write to Mr. Hoste and tell him I'll go somewhere else."

Jeff was delighted. "Good. You deserve an easier place to work after all you've done here."

"If nothing happens on this one final trip," Fraser hesitated in mid-sentence, "maybe you and I can go live like human beings in Tengyueh or Paoshan or somewhere. How would that be?"

Jeff grinned. "Sounds good to me. I'm ready to quit this business. I guess I can go to a few more villages."

Since Fraser was including him in his plans, Jeff couldn't just tell him he wanted to leave him. Not right now when Fraser was looking stronger and more hopeful again. Maybe there'd be an opportunity to bring it up later. He guessed he could manage one more trip.

The weather made this trip better than the previous ones Jeff had taken. Sunshine bathed the mountain slopes in changing patterns of light. Wild flowers waved their pink and yellow heads in the breeze.

The travelers headed west into the mountains. It was hard for Jeff to tell one place from another; all were mountainous, all were small thatched villages, all were primitive.

The village they stopped at the third evening was no different from the others Jeff and Fraser visited. The Lisu were friendly. They were also enthusiastic, willing to listen, and intelligent. But so far they did not seem eager to become believers in Jesus Christ. They just liked to have a foreigner with them for entertainment or something. Well, he was tired of being somebody's entertainment.

All the next day James taught reading to those who crowded into the tiny house. And singing. And basic health habits, like hand washing. The day wore on, the afternoon heat punctuated only by the occasional cluck of a chicken or growl of a mangy dog. With Lisu crowding around Fraser all day long, the house was stifling. It'd be better outside away from the village where there was always a wind through the pine trees. No one was paying any attention to him anyway. They were listening to Fraser or learning to read. Even Fraser seemed to have forgotten he was there. He'd go for a walk.

No one was watching him. Quickly he pulled out his tape player from under his sleeping bag where he stored it at night in case of pickpockets, clipped it to the front of his pants where it was covered by the loose Chinese jacket, and wandered out toward the path.

Soon Jeff was well clear of the village. The path wound around the hills, over rocks, between scrubby bushes. Mountains merged into mountains everywhere. As always, a band of mist hovered at the 6000-foot level. Above that poked the heads of the tallest peaks, straining to reach the clear blue sky above the fog. It was a day to smell, taste, experience with every pore of a person's being.

Jeff pulled out his cassette and put on the headphones. Here he could turn the volume up high. There was no one to keep telling him, "Don't have it too loud," like his mom would do if he were at home. Ah, this was better than staying inside bamboo walls. He breathed deeply, then blew his hair off his forehead.

Jeff lost himself in the sound from the Walkman, singing along with it, matching his step to the rhythm of the music. His eye caught sight of a hawk swooping down to the patch of trees to his right. But he saw or heard little else. Gradually, however, he became aware of a vibration on the ground — more a feel than a sound. Someone was coming!

At that point the trail squeezed between rocks less than a foot and a half apart. Behind the rocky outcropping on the left the mountainside rose almost straight up. Beyond the rocks on the right, it plunged sharply downwards to a valley too far below to calculate. No room for passing.

The brown-haired boy stretched to see the approaching party. A man was riding a horse, another man walking beside him. And it looked like someone or something was on the horse behind the rider. They were coming surprisingly quickly. Jeff looked around for some place to get out of the way.

Suddenly Jeff remembered his cassette player. He yanked the headphones from his ears and jammed the player back under his jacket. His hand was still in motion as the horse and men filled the path in front of him.

At sight of the rider's face Jeff's breath caught midway, and his stomach lurched. *Liang Tingwu!* The fat man's thin servant led the way, nervously grasping the reins. Jeff jumped to the left and scrambled onto a rock to be out of the way. At the sudden motion the horse bolted, sending the figure behind Liang tumbling. With a whimper-like cry, the dumped passenger hit the ground face first, immediately rolling over to reveal large, terrified eyes.

A girl! A Lisu girl, judging from her costume, thought Jeff. *Probably another case of this guy taking whoever he wants for himself.* The girl's hands were tied, Jeff noticed with disgust. *No wonder she couldn't hold on when the horse lurched.*

Old 'Crab-Face' was yelling now and the girl propped herself up on one elbow, struggling to get to her feet. Instantly, the servant, repeating the commands shouted by the boss, lifted his foot to enforce his orders. Before he could kick the fallen girl Jeff jumped onto the path. He landed just behind the servant, grabbed the man around the chest and pulled him backwards.

The girl was sitting upright now, and Jeff glanced her way. "Nyio-sa-mei!" He recognized her now. She was taller than last time he'd seen her, and her dirty face was streaked with tears. Using every muscle fiber, Jeff struggled to hold onto the servant, who was just a little taller than Jeff and amazingly strong. Though within seconds the wiry Chinese man had wriggled free, Jeff managed to hold him back just long enough for Nyio-sa-mei to get to her feet.

Liang Tingwu had slid off the horse, and now he faced Jeff, whip drawn in his hand. He was shouting and pointing, black eyes squeezed narrow with anger. As Jeff reached out to steady the trembling Lisu girl, Liang waved the whip menacingly. The path was too narrow to sidestep him. There was no sense turning around and running — a man on a horse could catch up to him in no time. And unless the overlord and his servant moved on and allowed him to go, he was trapped.

Suddenly Jeff realized the wire from his head-phones was hanging beneath his short jacket. He jabbed at it, hoping to tuck it in without looking too obvious. Too late! Liang Tingwu grabbed the wire and found the black object attached to it. He yanked it from Jeff's waist and pointed a finger with a long nail straight at Jeff's nose. He was saying something, shouting, but Jeff couldn't reply. His mouth was dry as powder, his tongue wouldn't move. He stared, speechless.

ELEVEN

Escape

It had all happened within seconds, and only now was Jeff aware of the fear stiffening every part of his body and making his heart pound. Sickeningly, the danger of his situation dawned on him. Not only was he helping a despised Lisu against the powerful Chinese who had her, but he had a dangerous-looking foreign device with him which probably linked him to the enemy British. He and Fraser might both be in big trouble. And he couldn't even explain. His lips stuck together and his mouth was dry. He had to try something. *Lord, help!* Never had he prayed more sincerely — never.

With a shaking hand Jeff reached out one finger to touch the player as it lay in the overlord's hands. To his surprise, the big man did not pull it back but stood watching to see what Jeff would do. "Okay, okay. I'll show you." Jeff tried to smile. He pressed the "Play" button and disconnected the earphones forcing the sound to come from the built-in speaker at the back. The man said nothing, watching and waiting. A few bars of music broke the tense air, echoing off the mountainside and across the abyss to infinity.

"Here. I know something you'll understand. Quickly, Jeff ran the tape ahead to the spot where James had recorded the Bible verse in Chinese and Lisu.

"You listen to this." Jeff kept his eyes riveted on the man's rigid face, hardly daring to breathe. The Chinese listened, face set in harsh lines, revealing nothing.

"It's the big teacher," Jeff told him, holding his hand up to indicate a tall man. He used the name the Lisu had given James, "Elder Brother Number Three, that's who it is."

The Chinese nodded. He recognized the voice of the big foreigner — the one he accused of being a British spy.

Liang Tingwu listened briefly, then as if hearing nothing that pleased him, he shoved the cassette player in Jeff's face for him to turn off, then stuffed it into the front pocket of his already bulging gown and began yelling again. The servant, at a command from his boss, jumped to find another rope in the saddlebags. Before Jeff could realize what he was up to, the man had looped it around Jeff's wrists.

"Hey, what —   No, oh, no you don't! You have no reason —Hey, undo this!" Jeff squirmed and kicked at the man's shins, but the servant was quick. In a matter of seconds, he had Jeff's hands tied securely in front of him. Now the servant shoved him into line behind the horse and forced him to walk.

Faltering under its double load, the horse picked its way down the trail, Liang seated in front, and Nyio-sa-mei bouncing roughly behind him. Jeff kept as wide a distance as he dared behind the horse, hoping for a chance to make a break. Behind Jeff, the servant scrambled and trotted nervously, giving high-pitched orders whenever Jeff stumbled on a rock or lagged behind.

Jeff was surprised how difficult it was to walk over the rough terrain with his hands tied. He wiggled his wrists angrily, trying to relieve the pressure of the ropes. "What are you doing with me?" he demanded. "Where are we going?"

Nyio-sa-mei said something Jeff took to be an answer, but it was meaningless to him. Still, the sound of her voice made him feel a bit better. She was probably even more angry and afraid than he was, Jeff realized. At least she had stopped crying with his being here. Maybe it helped her to feel she was not alone.

The sun bore a hole through his back with

its intensity, and Jeff longed for a drink. He didn't dare stop to complain, however. Step after step he dragged himself along behind Liang, his discomfort increasing by the hour. The sun had risen to its zenith and slid its way down the other side of the sky, but still they walked.

Surely they wouldn't walk all night, Jeff told himself. They'd stop soon. Surely. Anyway, maybe when they stopped, a man as wealthy as Liang would at least have some decent food for him. He repeated reassurances to himself as he stumbled along.

'Not being able to say anything that anyone understood was maddening. Though from time to time Nyio-sa-mei talked to Jeff softly, all he could do was grunt a reply or voice his own fears in English, which he knew did no good.

Jeff had no idea how long they had been traveling. Hours. More than a day maybe. Too long. The sun had long ago disappeared behind the mountains.

Drink, Jeff knew he had to have a drink! He was desperately hungry, but his thirst consumed him. His knees were like rubber, his feet as if they were heavy with mud. Eventually he felt he couldn't pick up his feet, not one more step.

Suddenly Jeff became aware that he was bouncing along in an even up-down rhythm. He opened his eyes. Someone must have lifted him onto the horse. Nyio-sa-mei was walking along behind now. Jeff closed his eyes again and drifted off to sleep under the horse's steady gait.

Hours or minutes later — Jeff couldn't tell — the noise of many voices stirred his brain to consciousness. The horse no longer moved under him. Quickly Jeff stiffened himself to alertness. Where was he? He had to pay attention. A large house stood beside him, surrounded with numerous sheds and other buildings. Obviously they had come to Liang's palace or whatever he called it. With the whole compound surrounded with a wide wall, Jeff had no way to get his bearings.

Servants poured out and scurried around at various tasks, welcoming Liang and caring for his horse. Everyone seemed to be jabbering at once, and Jeff was sure he was being thoroughly discussed.

As someone led him across the stone-paved courtyard toward one of the out buildings, Jeff turned to see Nyio-sa-mei being forced in another direction. He called her name, and she looked at him briefly, but a tug on his arm forced him forward. His wrists were swollen and his fingers numb from the rope that bound them. Once Jeff and his escort reached a mud-and-pole shed at the far end of the courtyard, Jeff was aimed at a low doorway and shoved into a dark room.

As Jeff stumbled inside, a narrow window running along the length of one wall let in just enough moonlight to illuminate rats scurrying out of sight. *Rats!* Jeff's skin crawled.

One comfort, the room had a raised platform in one corner for a bed, and the guard who led him to this rat hole threw a blanket onto the wooden platform. At least the prisoner wasn't expected to lie on the floor, with rats all over the place. The guard undid his wrists and with a few words was gone, locking the door behind him.

Jeff's mind had barely cleared from the confusion when the door opened again and another servant shoved a plate of food and a small pot of tea onto the floor, relocked the door and padded away.

Jeff drank and ate eagerly. He hadn't realized how good rice and tea could taste. He finished his meager supper and sank onto the makeshift bed, pulling one end of the blanket around him. His legs would barely move. Though his hands quite quickly regained their feeling and his fingers bent with slightly more ease as he limbered them into use, the rope marks on his wrists burned. And though he was exhausted, he couldn't fall asleep. His body trembling, he stared at the thatch roof above him. Now that the crisis was past — for the moment, anyway — he could think more reasonably about the situation.

So he was a prisoner at Liang's mansion. Actually it wasn't really a mansion. It was more like a big house surrounded by a collection of sheds, all enclosed by a wall. This was certainly not the impressive magistrate's compound he had seen from a distance in Tengyueh. They hadn't traveled that far, and there was no city around. Well, Liang would almost certainly have more than one residence, traveling throughout the region like he did.

Jeff was thankful that he was at least alive. And, to tell the truth, he wasn't really hurt, except for the rope burns which would go away in a day or two. And he had been fed. Was that a sign that Liang was going to treat him relatively well? Well for a prisoner, at least? Might it be so! Liang wouldn't really kill him, would he? Hopefully ol' Crab Face would just hold him for a few days and let him go — maybe just till he satisfied himself that this American upstart didn't mean any harm with his tape recorder.

Yes, his cassette player. Who knows what Liang would do with it? Even if he figured out how it worked and didn't break it, which was questionable, he'd never give it back. Better just say goodbye to it. He'd have to think of some way to tell his parents what happened to it. What's more, just the fact that he had it at all might be enough to get James into a lot of trouble. *Look where it got me!* thought Jeff. *In this rat-infested cell — that's where!*

But it was James that he worried about. What if James would get kicked out of Tantsah again? He was discouraged enough as it was.

What bothered Jeff most was that this was all his fault. He shouldn't be here. Suddenly a thought crystallized: If he ever got out of prison, he would leave Fraser and find somewhere else to live until he could get back home. This was absolutely the end. No matter what Fraser said about his help, he was doing more harm than good. If he had ever thought of carrying on with Fraser for the rest of this trip, he dropped the idea. No more. He would just come out and tell Fraser he was leaving, and that would be that.

Somehow the resolution had a calming effect. Tomorrow he would worry about getting out of here. For now, just planning made him feel better. Gradually his muscles relaxed, and he fell into a restless sleep.

The darkness of his room made it difficult to tell how time was passing. The ever-active rodent population kept waking him, leaving him wide-eyed and feeling creepy for perhaps an hour at a time, worrying that a rat might crawl up his blanket and over him. Every time he thought about it, he would shudder and pull the blanket around his ears. The night seemed forever.

Even after dawn, the time dragged. It had been light for several hours, Jeff guessed, before the man he thought of as the 'delivery man' deposited another plate of food and pot of tea inside his door.

Jeff ate all of his breakfast, though he didn't know what the dark, slightly slippery bits in it were. If he was going to get out of here, he'd need all the strength he could get. Some time later on, another meal appeared, this time, with a little green vegetable and two pieces of gingered fried pork on the rice.

Jeff's mind tested one idea after another for an escape. He had nothing with him to cut or shovel with. He wouldn't have been able to break out that way, anyway, judging from the strength of the walls and floor. The window was too high to reach and too narrow to allow his body through.

Was J. O. looking for him? Did he even know he was missing? He was probably so busy teaching the Lisu to read and sing, and writing down sounds that he didn't realize Jeff was even gone. That one-track Britisher would be so involved in his work, he probably wouldn't miss him. But even if James was looking, he'd have no idea where to find him, Jeff realized. He'd never dream what happened. No, Jeff was on his own. The next day a meal appeared again at his door. This time, the door opened quickly and the 'delivery boy' slipped inside and closed the door nervously behind him.

Jeff got a closer look now. It was not yesterday's food carrier, but Liang's personal thin-faced servant who had accompanied him on all his trips and who had brought Jeff here. Anger and fear immediately rose to Jeff's stomach, lacing it into a tight mesh.

But then Jeff saw the man's expression. It was softer, apologetic, almost kind. He stared in disbelief at the man who clasped and unclasped his fists and glanced to the window and all around the room before he spoke in low, excited tones. Over and over he repeated something, changing his gestures and facial expressions until Jeff understood.

He was helping Jeff escape!

Now that Jeff caught the drift of what the thin man had in mind, he shoved the last few bites of rice into his mouth, picked up his jacket and nodded at his would-be savior, who surprised Jeff with a fleeting, nervous smile.

"Which way?" he said, desperately trying to make the man understand. "Which way should I go?"

The man waved his arm toward the south, giving a few more instructions and held up five fingers.

"Okay, I understand. I'm to wait five minutes, then go and head that way. Okay." The man was shaking, Jeff noticed sympathetically. He was probably going to get in big trouble for letting Jeff go. If he was nervous on the trail, obeying Liang's orders, think how scared he must be now when he goes against them! Jeff forced a smile to his face, and said one of the few Chinese words he had learned: *"Shieh-Shieh"* — at least that's the way it sounded to him — "Thank you."

The man threw him one fleeting look of good will, opened the door and turned to yell at him before he banged the door shut and stomped off.

Jeff smiled. *That sounds convincing,* he thought.

Tense, the prisoner waited what he thought would be about five minutes, then he opened the door,which had been left unlocked, saw no one around, and crept along the side of the building toward the compound gate. The courtyard seemed empty — the servant must have created some kind of a stir inside to give him a chance to get away. He dashed for the gate and, once outside the wall that surrounded Liang's estate, he broke into a run.

The path the servant had indicated led back toward the villages where Jeff and Fraser had been visiting. It lay across open plain for a mile or more before the road narrowed to a path winding in and out of rocks again. Jeff sprinted across the open area. Once he began climbing, his progress was slower. He ran when he could, climbing quickly ahead and upward when he had to. He didn't dare slow down. By now Liang and his men would be out looking for him if the servant had given the alarm that he had fled. He kept watching for clumps of rocks or bushes that he could hide behind if necessary.

After an hour or two Jeff was stumbling. He

was pretty sure he'd gotten a head start on Liang and his men. They wouldn't be able to find him for a while. He had to rest. His chest was burning, and he needed to catch his breath.

And how he needed a drink! His mouth was cracking at the corners from dryness, and his tongue wouldn't move. A wide spot studded with clumpy shrubs spread out beside a stream to his left. Using the bushes for cover, Jeff half crawled toward the ribbon of water and dropped all the way onto his hands and knees to drink. *Oooh, did that taste good!* He half walked then to a spot hidden from the path and collapsed onto the ground to catch his breath.

Where was he going? He hadn't really given himself time to think about that, he'd been so thankful to escape from Liang. Now he'd better make some plans. If he kept on as he was, he'd probably come to a town of some kind eventually, that's probably why the servant had directed him that way. Then what?

It wouldn't help him get home, of course. He knew that. No one but Zeke could do that. But if he could find a bigger town, he might at least find some other Americans or English and a decent place to live while he waited to be rescued.

There was no sense walking on and on to meet up with Fraser. Jeff couldn't stand one more day tramping around with that idealist. Or staying in one more filthy Lisu village. James was probably too far on ahead by now anyway. If only he had some idea which direction led to civilization!

As Jeff sat on the ground against the brambles, he pulled his knees under his chin and gave in to the hopelessness of his situation. All the fear and anger he'd suppressed for the last days came to a head. He swallowed hard to hold the tears back. No use. His face twisted as tears welled up along his lower eyelids and spilled down his cheeks.

Wiping the wet away with the back of his hand, Jeff thought of the danger he was in with Liang looking for him. And the impossibility of going home. Frustration brought new tears as he remembered the cassette player he'd lost — to a man who couldn't even use it! He wiped his contorted and reddened face unconsciously against his shoulder. What a mess he had gotten himself into!

Some adventure! Misery, that's what his time with Fraser had been — days spent tramping, slipping, climbing, being robbed, getting injured, shot at, with nothing but rice to eat and no one for company but a dedicated genius with a one-track mind, so absorbed in his work he hardly noticed you. Seldom in his life had Jeff been so miserable. He couldn't live like this another day, he just couldn't!

Finally Jeff fell into an exhausted sleep. When he awoke, he got up stiffly and limped to the river, bent down and splashed his face and hair with water. Feeling better, he started to climb back up the steep bank to the path. Suddenly a sound made him stop short. Humming! A deep, melodic hum interspersed with la-la-la's. Who else but J. O. Fraser! "James!" Jeff tried hard to suppress the tears threatening to spill down his face again.

"Jeff, Jeffrey, is that you."

"Yes, I'm down here."

In a few minutes Fraser had clambered down the mountainside to meet him and was helping him up to the path, where a horse was cropping the grass beside the trail.

"Am I glad to find you! I left as soon as I heard about your run-in with Liang Tingwu. That was two or three days ago. Are you all right?"

Jeff caught his breath. "Yeah, yes, thanks; I'm all right. My wrists are still a bit sore, but they're healing."

Fraser dug in his saddlebags for a jar of Lisu honey he had brought with him and a ball of Chinese steamed bread. While Jeff ate, he tried to explain to James the events of the past three days. "How did you know where to find me?"

"When it got dark and you still hadn't come back to the village, I got suspicious, of course, and we searched the area around the house, but there was no sign of you. There wasn't much else I could do that night. The next day a man

from Atemesia Plain, the village just north of
where we were, came around and said he'd seen
Liang go through his village the day before with
two young people with him; one a Lisu girl and
one a foreign boy dressed in Chinese clothes."

"Yeah, Liang's got Nyio-sa-mei too. I didn't see
her again after we got to his place; so I don't
know what he's done with her."

"Well, I found out which direction he was going
and started out after you. The headman of the
village lent me his horse here. I'm glad I heard
you down there by the river — I'd been scanning
the road and the river all along the way."

"You've been riding all this time? Must be two
or three days at least — I've lost track. You mean
you've spent all this time looking for me?"

"Yes, I started out right away, and I stopped
only for short rest stops and to let the horse
eat and drink."

Jeff let out a deep breath. "You were heading
the other direction. We'd gone back towards
Tantsah. So you had to backtrack to find me."

"That's right. But we can soon make it up
again. We'll just walk a few days extra. What
else could I do? Did you think I'd just let somebody capture you?"

Jeff wagged his head no and was quiet for
a moment. Maybe he'd been wrong about Fraser.
Maybe he did care about him, about other things
besides his work. "Thank you. Thank you very

much. I — I hate to be such a nuisance."

"Nonsense. I told you I need your company."

He gulped and ran his fingers through his hair. *Might as well go on and tell him the whole thing,* Jeff thought. "Mr. Fraser, I've got something to tell you. Please don't take this personally. I really like you — as a friend. And I like your mountains and stuff — they're beautiful. And I like the Lisu people I've met. Most of them are friendly and smart. It's nothing against any of that — but," he took a deep breath, "I don't like living here. I'm sick and tired of eating rice and vegetables, climbing mountains all day, being attacked, and all for nothing. I mean, the Lisu aren't really believing in Jesus for all your efforts." He glanced up to see Fraser's reaction. His face showed nothing.

Jeff continued. "Besides, after this, I've probably messed things up for you worse than ever. I appreciate all you've done for me, I really do, but I want to leave. I can't go on with you. If you're going to leave Lisu work and go to the city, I'll stay. I'd really like to be able to do that. But if not, just tell me how to get to a consulate or ambassador or something where I can get some help. Or at least I could live with them in the meantime, and it'd be better than here." There, he'd said it. Jeff took a deep breath and waited for a response.

Fraser said nothing for a long while.

Jeff interrupted the silence. "You're not going to keep on here anyway, are you? I mean, you're going to leave the mountains soon, aren't you? Then we can both go together."

Fraser leaned his head back against a rock and closed his eyes. "I understand how you feel, Jeffrey. I don't blame you. Especially after this — you barely escaped with your life. No wonder you want to get as far away from here as possible!" He handed Jeff a handful of raisins he had brought along. "You have been a help to me, a good companion to live and travel with. I'm glad for your company. But I know you need to get back home — however you do that." He kept his eyes closed, and Jeff was glad he didn't have to answer that point.

"I tell you what. Much as I hate to see you go, I'll help you. But you can't just go on your own — you'd never make it. Stay with me as we make our way southward again. A little while longer. We'll visit like we've been doing, at the villages along the way. I've got to give them one last chance ...."

Fraser continued. "Anyway, we'll carry on southward toward the Burma border. Then when we get to Burma, I'll send a message to Ba Thaw and have him come and get you. He can take you into Rangoon and see that you get looked after. You'll find life much easier there."

Jeff hesitated. "No, I don't think so. No more.

I have —"

Fraser stopped him. "Jeffrey, be sensible. You can't just go off by yourself. Which way would you go? Where? How would you live along the way? And what if Liang finds you again?"

Jeff realized Fraser was right. He nodded. "Okay. Just till we get to Burma. I guess I can wait that long."

"Let's get going and see if we can cover a couple more miles before we camp for the night. We've got a long way to go."

The next day or so blurred together in Jeff's mind. One village was the same as another. In every one they sat and talked, James reading and explaining the Bible to them and answering their questions. They always sang, and often James taught them another prayer or a new hymn. Sometimes they were sick, and he gave them medicine and prayed for them. Then they traveled on to the next place. All the same.

By the third night after Jeff's meeting with Fraser the two of them stopped in another village after a long day of hill-tramping. They were welcomed by chickens, dogs, pigs and people alike, all eager to announce the arrival of Elder Brother Three and his "Found-by-the-Road" friend. Jeff was glad of the meal the hostess dished out.

After supper the neighbors crowded into the smoke-filled shack and listened attentively as James preached. They wanted to sing again the songs he had taught them on a previous visit, and they clapped and laughed their way through one after another. In a corner near the flickering pitch light five or six boys gathered around Jeff trying to learn to read. Jeff pronounced the sounds of each letter over and over, though he still didn't understand the words they spelled. The hostess, finished with her kitchen clean-up, sat down on the log beside Jeff and watched, her jewelry dangling and clanking as she moved. "It's a wonder she can straighten her neck with all that metal on it," Jeff said to Fraser.

Finally, with pitch torches to guide them, neighbors made their way to their homes for the night. Jeff and James' host shooed away the chickens and moved a woven basket or two to make room on the floor for the two visitors to sleep. It was another useless visit — full and sort of fun, Jeff had to admit, but useless.

Still, Jeff felt a little more up than he expected as he watched the shadows play on the soot-blackened roof from the smoldering hearth. He had been a little bit a part of what went on tonight. That felt good.

TWELVE
Decision

Jeff reached up to slap the mosquito that was nibbling his face when he realized Fraser was shaking him awake. "We'll have to stay here another day, it looks like," Fraser explained. "One family wants to believe. I'm going right now to see them."

"D'you have to go right now? Can't you even wait for breakfast? Oh, never mind!" Jeff crawled out from under his blanket and quickly pulled on his clothes, scrambling out the door and down the path after the long-legged Britisher. *What a guy!* Jeff thought grumpily.

All day Fraser stayed and explained to the family what being a Christian meant. They all enjoyed some kind of tubers, roasted in the hot embers, as questions and answers went back and forth pingpong style.

"They say they understand very well," Fraser
told Jeff as they trudged back to the place they
were staying as the sun cast long, golden fingers
across the landscape.

"They must understand — and believe," Jeff
responded eagerly. "Otherwise they wouldn't have
pulled down their demon shelves. Right?"

"Right," James agreed as he ducked to miss
an overhanging branch. He slithered down a final
bank, Jeff right behind him, and they were
"home."

James seemed pleased, of course, how the day
had gone. Still, as the day faded, he went quietly
about his routine, saying little. Jeff could understand
that — Fraser wouldn't want to get too excited
in case it didn't happen again. That night he sat
by the fire as usual, letting people come to him
and ask for his help, but not making any unusual
effort to get others to believe.

"I'm not going to try to persuade the Lisu to
become Christians," he explained to Jeff as they
settled under their blankets for the night. "They'll
never last unless they turn to God themselves,
wholeheartedly, because they see a need to do
so, not because I urged them to."

Jeff was surprised, and a bit disappointed.
Fraser'd never get people to become Christians
this way!

But the following day, in spite of a drizzly

morning, they found the next village was even more ready. No sooner had they finished eating lunch, squatting on the floor around the fire, than people were arriving at the door asking James to pray with them. They wanted to "walk the Jesus way," they said. James talked with each one, tailoring his prayer to meet each person's need.

No sooner had James finished teaching that group of families than word came that another family wanted to believe too. And then another. And another from the surrounding area.

In village after village it was the same. "That makes fifteen families in all that have turned to God in the last few weeks," James told Jeff as they made their way through steady rain towards Burma.

Fifteen more followed at Cypress Hill, and twenty-four more in Turtle Village, including the widow to whom he was lending his horse, after that.

"I don't think I'll have to write headquarters about a move, after all," Fraser said, delight dancing in his eyes in spite of exhaustion.

Jeff felt a sudden wave of disappointment. No chance anymore of their moving to a city. He was glad, of course, that the Lisu were believing. It was good to see J. O. Fraser being rewarded for all his efforts. But now he'd never leave here. Jeff would have to go on his own — or stay in this end-of-nowhere place with Fraser.

"Trouble is, I can't be everywhere at once," Fraser mused as they walked along after leaving more Christians behind. "Someone needs to visit all these new converts over and over again and teach them — someone who could spend some time with them. They're still afraid of the spirits, of sickness and death and nature. It's like the mist is still hanging around them — lighter, not as fearsome, but still hanging on. There's still so much they need to learn. And I don't even have a Bible in their own language to give them."

They were wending their way down a narrow mountain path, enjoying the pink and mauve of wild rhododendrons dotting the hillside, when Fraser suddenly said, "Shhh!" and thrust his arm straight back to signal Jeff to slow down. Someone was sitting by the path up ahead.

"Better stay behind me," Fraser warned, "until we know who it is and what they're doing. Follow me."

As they approached, suddenly Fraser burst into a run and the waiting figure jumped up, running toward him.

"Ba Thaw! What are you doing here? Just the person I'd hoped to meet!"

"I've been traveling around these villages visiting the new believers."

Fraser laughed. "Perfect! You're the answer to my dilemma."

They talked for a while as Fraser pulled out a canteen of water and passed it around. Fraser told Ba Thaw how many villages had turned to God. "They still need to be taught, to have someone answer their questions, pray for them, encourage them, help them when they're afraid of the spirits. We've seen a great beginning, but there's still so much to do."

Ba Thaw laughed. "Well, I'd better hurry up, from the sounds of all that work you've got lined up for me." He wiped the water from his mouth and rearranged his shoulder bag. "I have some more copies of the catechism with me."

"Which reminds me," Fraser said. "We've got to get more of God's Word translated into Lisu to give the Lisu believers. At least one Gospel in Lisu. Let's work on that this coming summer. I'll go to Burma so you can help me. We'll translate the Gospel of Mark. I want to expand the catechism too and add a few more hymns."

"I agree. Be glad to help. Meanwhile I'll use what I have. Oh, speaking of printed things, you might be interested in this, Jeff. When I was visiting in Kachin territory over that way, I found a whole village ready to welcome me. No wild dogs, no arrows — they were actually looking for me, it seemed."

Jeff grinned. "That's a change! What happened?"

"That's just it. They showed me a paper they

wanted me to explain. It was an American Sunday school paper — small two-page affair with green border. They said a foreign boy gave it to them when they tried to rob the foreigners a few months ago. They've had it all this time hoping someone could tell them about it."

Jeff's mouth dropped. "My paper! I pulled that thing out of my pocket in desperation to save them from taking our shirts!"

"Yes, I had figured that. On the second page it had a few verses from Romans in a box with a decorative border around it; so I read the verses and translated them into Kachin. The line that got to them was, "The wages of sin is death, but the gift of God is eternal life" — you know the verse. That led to a great opportunity to go on and explain to them how Christ had died for them and wanted to give them power over the spirits. Eventually three from that village believed in Christ and burned their demon things."

Fraser looked over at Jeff, and a slow-spreading smile lit up his face. "Well, that was a worthwhile robbery, I say."

Jeff grinned. "I don't know about that, but I'm glad I had that paper in my pocket. Wow! That little thing led to three people actually becoming Christians. I can't believe it!"

"Again, the Word of God in language the people can understand, even though in this case it took Ba Thaw to translate it on the spot. See what I mean?" Fraser said, waving his arms in emphasis. "I hope we'll see more believers among the Kachin. Maybe as Christians they'll live peaceably with everyone else. Even Lisu."

"Hmm. That'd be news!"

As Ba Thaw got ready to separate and move on, Fraser put his hand on his arm. "There's one more thing I need to mention, Ba Thaw." Jeff felt his stomach tighten as he knew what was coming. "I promised Jeffrey you'd help him. He wants to get back home — to America. I don't know how he plans to do that, or if you can help in that, but I told him I'd have you take him across the border to Burma and get him to the British legation there. Maybe they can help him get home. If not, they can at least provide a better place to live in the meantime. This is no place for a boy, living with me. I promised him I'd ask ...."

Jeff cleared his throat and ran his fingers through his hair. "Uh — uh, Mr. Fraser," he licked his lips thoroughly, "uh, I don't know. I mean — well, it's true I don't like living like this, and I wish you'd work somewhere else; but now that all these people are becoming Christians, just what you've hoped for, and all —"

"I certainly won't be leaving now," Fraser said defensively, "if that's what you're hoping."

"No. I know. I don't expect you to. And, well, I think I should stay with you a little while longer."

Jeff could hardly believe what he was hearing himself say. But somehow he meant it.

Fraser looked at him, a long hard look that seemed to see right through Jeff. Jeff kicked a small pebble away from his toe.

"Are you sure, Jeffrey? We may not see Ba Thaw again for a while; this is your chance. If you want him to take you —"

Jeff spoke up now. "No, I'm sure. I'm staying with you as long as I'm — as I'm here."

Fraser shook Jeff's hand in a gigantic, enthusiastic handshake. "Thanks, friend." His sober eyes sparkled. "Thank you!"

Jeff hoped he'd made the right choice.

THIRTEEN
Surprise at Mottled Hill

"What's that?" Jeff said, staring at the activity on the path-scarred hill ahead of him.

"Something's going on — some kind of celebration by the looks of it."

Fraser and Jeff had left Tantsah a few days before to reach out in a wider sweep. They were walking in the shadow of the mountain range, approaching Mottled Hill, the first village Jeff had entered when he landed on the mountains of Lisuland.

"Listen," Jeff said, stopping suddenly. "Do you hear what I hear?"

Fraser nodded. "Singing. Bum ba-bum ba-bum de-dum-dum," he sang. "That's Ba Thaw's translation of 'What a Friend We Have in Jesus.' What on earth is going on here?"

He stepped out ahead of Jeff now, almost running up the mountainside, ignoring the path. Jeff followed. How long ago had it been when he wandered into this place, half-frozen and confused? Such a lot had happened since. But the village looked the same — same shacks squatting on patches of dirt leveled out of a vertical mountainside. Same pigs and chickens and tiny garden plots. But there was one big difference. He could see the focus of the celebration now — a little building made of woven bamboo mats topped with a thatched roof in the middle of the village.

"A church," Fraser called back to him excitedly, "the first Lisu church building in these mountains." Jeff approached the crowd milling about. They were putting the finishing touches on their creation, tamping down the dirt floor and adding long reeds for flooring. "They must have built this all themselves. I had no idea —" James talked to one man after another until he heard the whole story.

"They say shortly after so many Lisu began to believe, Ba Thaw came here and stayed for a few weeks and taught them. Fifty-one families believed, and he encouraged them to build a place of worship. I don't think he expected it to be this grand."

Jeff remembered very well how poor the village was. There was no question the chapel was bigger than any of the little houses around it. Stronger too, by the looks of the walls. And with a well-matted thatched roof. And, so far at least, it wasn't even full of smoke. "I guess you could call it 'grand,'" he said hesitantly.

"Oh, yes, by their standards this is a beautiful piece of architecture. I asked the men how they did it. I mean this would cost more than any of them have." Fraser was growing more excited by the minute. "They said everyone contributed something. Free labor, free land, free reeds and bamboo — they just all pitched in and gave what they had. Now, look at this place!"

A huge smile lit up Fraser's usually serious face. He was proud of the little woven building. No wonder. It really had cost a lot for people as poor as these were.

"Tonight they're going to start the dedication ceremony," Fraser continued. "We'll have to dress up for that."

That evening Jeff changed into clean pants and shirt and hurried along to the meeting with the crowd. Men and women from the hills all around filed along the narrow path into the village, large black turbans wound around their heads, earrings dangling, necklaces gleaming. Children pushed their way in to see, and girls giggled and huddled in clumps at the edges. Even the dogs got into the celebration, nosing their way among the visitors, hoping for a tidbit.

Clearly everyone was in a good mood. "Seems like Christmas," Jeff remarked. "I guess these are their best clothes."

"Absolutely. They don't get much excitement in their life way up here. This is a big occasion. Look at all that jewelry. And see those women? Notice those fancy colored stripes around the sleeves and those shells around the aprons. Those girls are dressed up!"

"Niyo-sah-mei's house was the first one over there on the left," Jeff said, pointing. "Of course she isn't here now — thanks to Liang," Jeff said angrily. He could feel the ropes on his wrists all over again, just remembering the incident. "But I wonder if her family will be taking part in the celebration."

"If they ever became Christians, they will be, I'm sure of that."

"I hope so — they might have some news of Nyio-sa-mei."

From all over the hills they came, lighting their way with pitch-burning torches, till the whole chapel was full of light.

"James! James Fraser!" an English-sounding voice called from somewhere in the crowd.

"It's Ba Thaw!" Fraser ran to greet his friend. "Well, if anyone deserves to be here at this celebration, you do," he told him. "I understand you were the one responsible for this building."

Ba Thaw shook his head, uncomfortable with

the credit. "No, no. I taught them, yes, but the people built this all of their own accord. They gave the supplies, the land, everything."

They pushed their way into the new building with the rest of the crowd. The aroma of new-cut grass and reeds permeated the air.

The floor space was full. Not one more body could squeeze in. All the overflow were standing outside, peering through the door, through cracks, through any tiny opening they could find. Everywhere Jeff looked along the wall, there were eyes peering through the woven bamboo. At the front a huge, raised rock held burning pine pitch.

Someone must have suggested a song, because before Jeff knew it everyone was singing. It wasn't one Jeff recognized, but the Lisu seemed to enjoy it immensely. They sang another song, and another. Now they broke into harmony, singing parts — just like a choir at home. This was really beautiful. Jeff thought of the contrast with the original attempts at "Jesus Loves Me" a year or so ago.

Then the leader began a sentence, and every-one joined in reciting together. Fraser leaned close to Jeff's ear and interpreted. "God our Father, Creator of Heaven and Earth," they prayed. "Creator of mankind, we are your children, we are followers of Jesus. Watch over us this day; don't let the evil spirits see us. We are trusting in Jesus. Amen."

Though they prayed several times during the evening, the words were always the same.

"That's one of the things we'll have to teach them," Fraser said later, "to pray in their own words about their own needs. But for now, I'm sure God is happy just to hear His children's voices."

Jeff laughed, remembering Mrs. Tsai's practical prayer for her pig. "They'll learn to pray like Ah-Do's mother. Then you'll hear some very original requests!"

The celebration continued all the next day. The women had woven branches and flowers into a welcome arch which each arriving guest must pass under. Church members lined both sides of the path at the edge of the arch, greeting each one as they entered. Sunshine and blossoms, colorful clothes and food luxuries made the atmosphere festive. On a giant outdoor barbecue a pig was roasting to feed the crowd, it's aroma tempting everyone who passed. Jeff inched closer for another whiff of it.

Close behind Jeff a girl giggled. The boy in jeans turned to see a familiar face. Nyio-sa-mei! She put her hands over her mouth in embarrassment, but the eyes that looked out at him twinkled with delight. He smiled at her.

"Nyio-sa-mei! I'm glad to see you. What are you doing here? I thought Liang took you."

Well, all right — so she couldn't understand. He had to say something! She nodded and chattered in turn.

Then Nyio-sa-mei grew serious. She looked around hesitantly. People milled everywhere, no one could expect to be alone. But in general people seemed to be busy with their own conversations. She motioned for Jeff to follow her.

Nyio-sa-mei crossed the yard to her house and motioned Jeff inside. Jeff had a funny feeling doing this the second time. He wasn't surprised now at the smoke filled interior and the lack of furnishings. The girl he had last seen with her face streaked with tears and her arms bound behind her went to the corner, rummaged in a basket, and produced a piece of paper. It was the piece of paper that had started all the ruckus on his first visit! Jeff grew uneasy.

Nyio-sa-mei wasn't finished. Opening a basket, she dug under some cloth and a bag of salt and pulled out something. With a smile of anticipation she held it out to Jeff with both hands. His cassette recorder! Here it was, along with the head phones, all apparently intact.

"How on earth —? Thank you. Thank you very much, but how did you get it?" He quickly checked out the buttons and the cassette. It still played. Everything seemed to be undamaged.

"It still works. I can't believe it. I wish you

could tell me —"

"I can." A man's voice behind Jeff interrupted. Ba Thaw stood in the doorway in his finest Lisu clothing, smiling. "I can help. Let me translate for you." He said something to Nyio-sa-mei, who began to pour out her story. Ba Thaw translated quickly.

"She says, after she saw you in the courtyard of the Chinese magistrate's house — Liang's place — she was taken to a room with his other wives. She was called in to see Liang several times. He finally figured out how the 'talking box' worked."

Ba Thaw looked at the girl and listened for several seconds. "She says he kept it with him in his possession and treated it carefully. But he played it over and over, especially the part of J. O. saying verses of Scripture. Then one day he called her in and told her she was free to go home. And that the big teacher in the talking box was not bad. The Lisu were free to believe whatever they liked."

Ba Thaw nodded as the girl continued, and a look of admiration broke over his face. He smiled at her and said something and then told Jeff, "She made excuses to delay leaving the house until he was busy with a visitor; then she walked boldly in to his private apartment and took the 'talking box' with her and carried it home, hoping to see you some day and return it. And here it is!"

Jeff was speechless for a moment. Then he grinned. "Good for you! Thank you. Thank you very much."

But Nyio-sa-mei wasn't finished. Ba Thaw translated: "That servant who let you go — she says he was kind to her too. He has no love for Liang; he's just afraid to disobey him. Apparently he was the first in the household to believe in Christ." Ba Thaw's face beamed.

"When Liang began to soften his attitude a little, word spread quickly," Ba Thaw explained. "So by the time you and James got back to the villages a week later, the Lisu had heard that there was a talking box with the voice of Elder Brother speaking Lisu and that the Chinese authorities had withdrawn their threats. So since there was nothing to stop them, they quickly unchained their faith. That's when the change came."

"Oh, one more thing," Jeff said to Ba Thaw, "ask her if she ever learned to read?"

Nyio-sa-mei smiled in reply, and Ba Thaw told Jeff, "She has. She started by learning the letters from that paper Liang took in the first place. And then when she came home, she continued working through a copy of the catechism that Fraser had left in another village and that her father had bartered to get. Every day she practiced. I helped her myself when I was here once."

Excitedly Nyio-sa-mei reached inside the folds of her apron and pulled out her handwritten copy of the catechism in Lisu script. Jeff leaned over her shoulder for a look. Sure enough — it was the little catechism in question-and-answer format that James had written, with simple teachings about the Christian faith. Jeff listened, amazed, as she began to read, rapidly and with ease, running her finger along each line.

Finally she stopped and beamed at him, a white, sparkling smile that changed her whole face.

She's really pretty, Jeff thought. *I never noticed it before, but she's actually pretty.* He noticed how clean she was compared to the day he saw her in the market, or even compared to their latest encounter just a few weeks ago. And how much more grown up she looked! In the last few weeks she had changed from a dirty child into a beautiful girl.

Jeff applauded her. "Good for you" He turned to Ba Thaw. "Did she ever become a Christian? And her family, what about them?"

"Oh yes, they all turned to Christ and destroyed their demon-worship stuff on my last visit."

Nyio-sa-mei was talking again. "She says," Ba Thaw informed Jeff, "that reading the little message on the scrap of paper helped her understand the Gospel. But —" He listened as Nyio-sa-mei said some more, shyly this time, her cheeks blushing and her eyes looking at the floor. "The thing that really made her want to believe was seeing you stick up for her in front of Liang that day in Tengyueh. No one ever sticks up for the Lisu. She was impressed that you would."

Jeff was speechless. He didn't know which was the most amazing — having his cassette player back in one piece or knowing that his reaction at Liang Tingwu's meanness had helped Nyio-sa-mei accept Christ. More wonderful was the fact that there were Christians among the Lisu in village after village, all over the mountains! He never expected to see his recorder again, let alone be a part of what God was doing in these mountains. A big knot swelled in his throat, and tears were suddenly making it hard to see.

As Jeff followed Ba Thaw out of the house, James bounced up behind him and put a long arm around his shoulder. "Isn't this wonderful? There're Christians here from all around. Wait till my prayer helpers hear about this!"

Jeff saw the old sparkle flash in his eyes again. "Of course, we'll have to revisit all these villages again as soon as possible. As soon as we leave here, we'll go back and visit each one."

Jeff groaned, dismissing the tears with the back of his hand. Another trek? "*We?* What d'you mean, *We?*" I didn't say I'd keep this up forever." He grinned at the tall man beside him. "I have to admit this mountain climbing sure has built up my leg muscles. But, again? So soon? It would be nice to stop and live a little." He didn't want to think about walking right now;

he was feeling unusually tired.

Jeff ate his share of roast pork and several heaped mounds of rice. Not till that evening towards bedtime did he feel ill. Not really ill. "I mean, it's not because of anything I ate," he told Fraser. "It's not my stomach. Just my head. I don't know ... I feel sort of dizzy."

"Here, lie down. Maybe you're over-tired. After all, we've had a lot of activity the last few weeks."

"Yeah, but it's not just that. I don't know what it is." Though he shook his head, he couldn't clear away the funny, drifting sensation that engulfed him. He lay back down, closed his eyes and tried to sleep.

Beside him Fraser settled, contentedly. "It's been a wonderful day. Amazing. I knew God was going to do it. I was praying for Lisu Christians all over these hills — and the folks in England have been praying. I must write and tell them the results their prayers have had. I think today we've seen the beginning. There's still a long way to go, but we've seen the beginning."

Jeff must have drifted off to sleep. When he awoke, he was looking at an oyster-white wall and grayish blue carpet. His head was still a bit foggy, but the intense dizziness had subsided. He was afraid to move. He looked around. This wasn't any Lisu hut. Not even China.   This ...

"Hey, where —? What am I doing here?" he asked, suddenly pulling himself to a sitting position.

Zeke came rushing over and helped him to his feet. "Oh, Jeff, I'm sorry. It happened again. Well, that is, not the same problem. This time it was —"

"Just a minute, just a minute. I don't care about the technical details. You mean something in that gismo went wrong again and catapulted me —"

"Crazy thing! Sorry.But you're all right, aren't you? Anything broken?"

Jeff tested his legs and arms gingerly. "No, I seem to be okay. My head's stopping its spinning now."

"Good. Then maybe we'd better go. I'll show you the rest another time. I must get Bob to fix that   crazy   connection between .... "

Obviously not open to hearing Jeff's story, Uncle Zeke talked on as they went down the long hallway to the elevator. Jeff pretended to listen, saying nothing. He reached in his pocket. Yes, it was still there. Whether anyone believed him or not, he had to know for sure for himself. He pulled out his tape player and put the head-phones on his ears. *Still playing,* he thought. The final bars of the title song ended and after a second of silence came a deep English voice saying something in Chinese, then in Lisu. Then came Lisu songs. And a whistle. Jeff grinned. There was his proof.

Zeke turned to see Jeff, smiling and humming.

"What are you doing? Hurry up."

Jeff, sure that he would never be the same again, ran a couple of steps to catch his uncle. "Yeah, sure," he said to get on his uncle's wavelength. "I'm just thinking what good batteries this thing has. Great little recorder here!"

Epilog

Except for Jeff Anderson, Liang Tingwu, and Nyio-sa-mei, all the people you met in this story are real. Though a few of the names have been changed, the living conditions, the places and events described are all genuine.

Moh Tingchang lived as a faithful witness for Christ in Hsingta. People from the mountains visited him when they came to town, asking questions and listening to him tell of God's power over evil. He helped hundreds of tribal people put their trust in the Lord Jesus.

Ba Thaw continued to visit Lisu villages and teach at believers' conferences and help with translation. He and Moh often traveled together, preaching on one mountain after another.

Mr. Fraser later married and had three

Epilog 201

daughters, who are now living in England.

J. O. Fraser died on September 25, 1938, in Paoshan, China. By that time the mountains of Lisuland were dotted all over with bamboo churches like that first one in Mottled Hill Village. The Lisu Christians attended Bible school and even sent out their own missionaries to other areas. Even thousands of Kachin came to know Christ, and today there are Christians among almost all the tribal groups of that area.

After Mr. Fraser's death other members of the China Inland Mission (now called the Overseas Missionary Fellowship) carried on the work he had begun. John and Isobel Kuhn were mainly responsible for teaching and preaching; Alan and Evelyn Crane and Allyn and Leila Cooke translated the Bible and prepared Bible lessons. Others spread the Gospel to North Thailand.

Though the Lisu had the New Testament in their own language by 1936, the first complete Bibles did not reach them until 1968. Members of the Overseas Missionary Fellowship are now translating a Bible dictionary into Lisu. The Orville Carlsons, formerly of OMF, are also deeply involved in translation work. Recently, the Chinese government recognized the "Fraser script" as the official Lisu written language.

In 1950 all missionaries had to leave China. But today in China, Burma, and North Thailand there are thousands of Lisu Christians. And they still love to sing! Nearly a century later, the music and the message which J. O. Fraser brought still echoes east of the misty mountains.

If you would like to know more about Mr. Fraser or the Lisu, you can write to Overseas Missionary Fellowship at one of the addresses listed on the copyright page of this book.